A SPARK OF MAGIC

MAGICAL SHORT STORIES, VOLUME THREE

T. THORN COYLE

All I could see at first was her shape: substantial thighs wrapped in a slim skirt, long legs, sharp padded shoulders, and a hat perched on waves of hair.

I could also tell that she was radiating power. The kind of power most people only notice as a sort of charisma. They know they're drawn in or repelled, but they can't quite tell you why. It has nothing to do with looks, or how much cash and flash a man has, and everything to do with magic.

A BRIEF INTRODUCTION FROM THE AUTHOR

Magic defies space and transcends time. These stories reach into the past, open up the present, and imagine the future.

Magicians, peep show dancers, lonely men, lost girls, and Death Herself walk through these magical tales.

Every single story in this collection comes from my wishes for a more magical world. These stories evoke the longing of a broken heart, a whispered prayer, a candle lit, a heartfelt wish, and the sort of retribution sometimes only magic brings.

And we all know, that life without magic is a life without wonder.

Here's a collection of five stories, all written with the support of my amazing Patreon friends. Some of these short tales have appeared in other collections, some not, but nonetheless these five stories all wanted to live together beneath one cover.

So here they are: past, present, and future.

I hope you enjoy reading these as much as I enjoyed writing them.

Make a wish.

T. Thorn Coyle
  Portland, Oregon
  2020

THE MAGIC AROUND HER

A RON MCGEE MAGICAL ASSOCIATION STORY

The day she walked into the bar, I was hurting. And I had been, for a very long time...

It was a sunny Saturday afternoon in Pasadena. The bar was only half full because Terry was working the barbecue, drawing people to the tiny concrete patio out back. The men wore straw trilbies to shade their eyes, and light shirts to ward off the heat.

The women? They stayed in the bar, in the cooler shadows, sundresses fanned around their pretty dark legs.

The front and back doors were both open to the late afternoon summer sun, casting wedges of golden light on the scarred wood floors, shimmering across pristine bottles on the shelves at the back of the wood bar. There was no mirror there, but I swear Johnson had eyes on the back of his head if trouble walked through the door.

I'd been outside earlier, sipping on a beer, waiting for my late lunch to be done cooking. A few of the usuals were in the house, the ones I hung out with, playing cards, catching the occasional show. Bill. Jones. Carmine. Louis. Were they friends? I think so. Did I really know them? Not so much.

Didn't really know anybody much these days.

The men's voices rumbled and rose as the cards snapped onto the round wood table where a game was in progress. They were likely warming up with a friendly round of gin rummy.

Everyone else must have taken the Big Red Cars to the beach. Or they were working, like I should be. Instead, I was sitting at on the burgundy leatherette bar stool permanently dented by my muscled posterior, down near the end of the long sweep of mahogany bar.

My brown fedora took up the barstool next to me.

The low murmur of voices from couples at some of the two tops was punctuated by the sharp laughter and muffled swearing from my four friends.

Usually I would be with the game. Not today, though. My heart just wasn't in it. I'd declined the invitation, once I'd gotten my barbecue, and taken some teasing about my dark moods.

Today, my mind was full, and my belly? I was stuffing it, too. Stuffing away regret along with barbecued pork. If I wasn't careful, my six-two frame was going to fill out around the middle in ways that would just slow me down.

I didn't need to slow down any more than I was these days.

The brand new Filben Maestro clicked and whirred, long arm grabbing another black disc from its stack of 78s. Dinah Washington started crooning. Johnson was so proud the day the delivery men hauled that jukebox into place, he'd bought everyone in the house a beer.

My fingers sticky with tangy sauce, I made short work of the pile of pork ribs that were always cooking on sunny weekends outside this tidy joint in the old part of Pasadena.

The thin paper napkins weren't quite up to the job, but I wasn't willing to leave my bourbon in order to go wash my hands.

Johnson was filling a pint glass from the tap.

He occasionally glanced at me, like he was worried about something. I hoped it wasn't me. Bartenders shouldn't worry about their customers, even regulars. But Johnson and I had been friends ever since I walked through the front door of his bar six years ago, asking if he'd ordered two kegs or just one.

These days, I was a paperhound, writing columns and news for the *Pasadena Voice*, the local black rag that kept up on community gossip, music, police reports, and sometimes, actual news. The kind of news the *LA Times* didn't care to report.

There was a concert I was planning to take in later. Our Arts reporter was out of town and all the odd jobs still fell to me. I didn't much mind. A concert would keep me away from my bed. Away from the nightmares dogging my brain with images I couldn't quite decipher, but could feel to the marrow of my bones.

I was trying a third round with the crappy napkins, shredding them over my fingers as they caught on Terry's special sauce, when a shadow cut through the oblongs of sunlight coming through the door. All I could see at first was her shape: substantial thighs wrapped in a slim skirt, long legs, sharp padded shoulders, and a hat perched on waves of hair.

I could also tell that she was radiating power. The kind of power most people only notice as a sort of charisma. They know they're drawn in or repelled, but they can't quite tell you why. It has nothing to do with looks, or how much cash and flash a man has, and everything to do with magic.

Shit.

As she entered, I could see she wore a navy suit that skimmed her impressive figure, cupping those thick thighs and a little mound of belly before nipping in at the waist and tapering out again to skim her breasts. Gold-plated brooch on one lapel. Red pillbox at an angle on those dark, dark, waves of hair. It matched the red of her T-strap shoes.

Her skin was deep, with rich undertones picked up by that hat, and by the red stain that traced her round lips.

She glanced around the bar, not like she was looking for anybody, just assessing. Then she walked right toward me.

Her heels struck the wood floors like castanets. I wished I had clean hands.

"Mr. McGee?" Her voice was like honey pouring over gravel.

Swiping at my mouth and hands with yet another napkin, I shoved the stool back and stood. She was smaller than I'd thought at first, but she still loomed large. The magic crackled around her, and once again I wondered how the hell nobody saw it.

And I wondered where she came from.

She held out her hand.

I gestured toward the basket of pork bones with my sticky hands, fingers splayed in explanation. Her red mouth quirked up to the left.

"I'll wait."

Okay. An order to go wash my hands. I didn't usually take orders from anyone, but my momma taught me not to be rude, either. Besides, I wasn't sure yet that this woman couldn't fry me where I stood.

In the tiny men's room, I washed my hands, then splashed some water on my face. Advancing the towel on the big wall roller, I patted everything dry. My mind was even more full, now. Who was she, what did she want, and how had she found me today of all days?

And why?

I glanced at myself in the mirror above the porcelain sink. A nice face, but nothing to write home about. A man who had tried to blend in for years—whether as a delivery man or the reporter leaning against the back wall, half obscured by a potted palm —had just been noticed by a creature who would always stand out, even if she was trying not to.

And she knew something. That was clear.

By the time I returned, she was sitting at a two top, with a gin and tonic at her elbow. Her eyes followed me, and she inclined her head toward the other chair at the little wooden table.

Still calling the shots. Okay. I grabbed my finger of bourbon from the bar and joined her.

She smelled of lilac soap and bonfires at the beach. Strange combination, but it suited her, somehow.

"Your name is?"

"Rose Clemmons." Her lips left a faint half moon of red on the clear glass.

I took a sip of my bourbon and leaned forward in my chair.

"What do you want?"

Her power shifted at the question, adjusting itself around her body. She leaned in toward me, scent of lilac soap caressing my face. I wanted to fall into her, let her surround me, comfort me, take my pain away.

"That's right," she said. "I'm here to ask what it is *you* want. You've been telegraphing all over town today, Mr. McGee."

She leaned back in her chair again, taking away some of the comfort on offer.

Somehow, that made me mad. How dare she? My hands clenched on the tabletop, and I threw back the rest of my bourbon. It burned all the way down to my belly.

"Who are you?" I asked.

She smiled again, with that same left-tilted quirk of the lips. "I thought I told you already. My name is Rose."

"Well, Rose who smells like lilacs, I think you know I wasn't asking after your name."

Her beautiful face set into harsh planes at that. The magic grew very still around her, and her eyes went flat.

I squeezed up to keep from pissing my slacks.

"You have no cause to question me, Ron McGee."

"I do if you come to my place and start threatening me. And how do you know my name? Who's been talking?"

She laughed at that, her eyes growing warm again, face cracking open with delight. How could anyone be that changeable? That in touch with her emotions? I could tell the laugh was real, because of her eyes and because the magic was in motion once again.

"You've been telling me yourself, Mr. McGee. You are a remarkably easy man to track down."

Her laughter relaxed me, even though her words didn't ease my mind. No longer terrified, I still needed to pee, and excused myself to do so. And to buy myself some time.

There hadn't been a magic worker in Pasadena in ten years. Not that I knew of. And there hadn't been a woman I'd found this attractive in seven. I'd grown used to being alone. Used to hanging out with my buddies here, playing cards. Used to eating supper at the bar. Used to chasing down stories that weren't that interesting, in the hopes that I'd stumble across something real again.

Just like I used to. Back then. Back when I had power like the stuff rolling around Rose Clemmons like so much perfume. She made it look easy, to carry that kind of power.

I knew it wasn't. At least it never was for me. That's why I gave it up. Until I missed it. But then I was too afraid to get it back. And the dreams weren't helping. Matter of fact, I needed help with those dreams. They were going to eat me alive. Or worse, they were going to come true.

When I returned, she was sitting calmly at the table, a fresh bourbon glowing golden orange at my place. She'd gotten us cups of water, too. I should probably drink some.

"I apologize, Rose Clemmons. I haven't been myself for a long time. You coming into my place like this"—I lowered my voice—"all tingling with magic, knowing things about me...makes me a little nervous."

She laughed again, more softly this time. "More than a little nervous, I'd say. Further proof of what you are. Ordinary people just take what I offer and thank me. Only folks like you fight back."

It was my turn to grow completely still. I didn't want this. I so did not want this. I'd given it up for a reason, several reasons, several very dangerous, humiliating reasons, that all came crashing back.

There was a reason I hung out here, among ordinary people, trying to do ordinary things, even while looking for proof that the extraordinary was still out there. I wanted to find it. I didn't want to find it. Both of those were true.

But mostly, I didn't want it to find me.

She just looked at me. A being whose magic was rooted in the strength of compassion. How was that even possible? I didn't know beings like her even existed.

I looked away, tears pricking at the back of my eyes.

It isn't easy being seen.

"I don't understand," I said, staring at my drink.

She reached a hand across the table, palm up, an offering. I didn't take it. Took a sip of bourbon instead.

"I'm a Suffering Woman," she finally said.

"You don't..."

"We do."

You don't exist, was what I had barely stopped myself from blurting out. The Suffering Men only existed in stories, like the ones my auntie told. Their magic eased the pain of those who needed it.

"Why don't they help everyone?" I used to ask.

"Because there aren't enough of them to go around," my auntie said. "And some people clutch their suffering like diamonds, not willing to let go."

That last part never made sense to me as a child. It sure made good sense now. My suffering was all that was left of the disaster I'd wrought. And without suffering, it was too easy to just slide into this life of mine like the nightmares wouldn't happen. Like the omens just weren't real.

Her coming here proved it all.

"I can help you," she said.

Pitching my voice low, I leaned in again, staring at her eyes.

"Help me do what? Help me figure out that I can fuck this thing up, too? That I can't save a bunch of people living on the edge of danger? That I can fail again?"

Damn her compassionate eyes. Damn her lipsticked mouth, ready to speak more words of comfort.

I held up my hand to stop her. Drank some more. She sipped her G and T.

The reason Johnson's was my home away from home was its normalcy. Same reason I'd settled in Pasadena after it all went down. It was still familiar, still Los Angeles, but it was its own little protected enclave, nestled against the hills of Eagle Rock. The black population here was small, but that suited me just fine. The main thing that suited me, though? The lack of magic.

There were nightclubs in Beverly Hills that reeked with sorcery. And the occasional Crenshaw tavern where you'd find spell casters, witches, and the like. I wanted away from it all. I wanted to just live my life, and had been doing fine until the nightmares started six months ago.

I looked up at her. She just waited. Calm. Sipping her gin and tonic like she had nowhere else to be, and no one more interesting or hand-some to keep her company.

"You from Andre's?" I asked. A posh club in Century City, Andre's hosted big bands and top crooners. Money ran in and out of that place on a river of champagne. And sorcery was the currency everyone traded in. Or wanted to. Those who didn't have magic had connections, or looks, or very deep pockets.

"What if I am?" she asked, a bit more gravel than honey this time.

"Then I have nothing to say to you."

Andre's was the place it had all gone wrong. The place I'd almost died. I could still taste the terror of it in my mouth. I could smell the sorcery whirling around my head and wrapping up my body until I could barely move.

I had torn that sorcery to shreds, killing her in the process. My wife. My lover. My friend.

None of it had needed to happen, except that he wanted to show me that he had control. Lawrence Barlow. Dapper, debonair, and rich. Strongest magical bastard in the whole Los Angeles basin. But that wasn't enough for him. He wanted my wife, too.

But she hadn't wanted him.

That wasn't all of it, of course. Barlow was running cocaine out of back rooms, and likely running guns and women, too. All things that sorcerers like me had taken vows not to do. We weren't supposed to use offensive magic, either. Well, that night, I broke that vow.

That night, I let out everything I had and tore the place apart. Heard it took Andre six months to rebuild. I felt only mildly badly about that. Andre's a pretty good man, and he runs a swank club. Helps a lot of people. But he also let people like Barlow take over a few too many things. Some lessons we learn the hard way.

Like I learned the night Betty died.

We'd been fighting off his sorcery, back to back, her high notes weaving up above my low, my dark velvet mixing with her satin.

But Barlow and his people were too strong. Too fierce. Too underhanded. Strong as Betty and I were, we couldn't combat that much dirty fighting. So I lost it. My rage ripped it all to shreds.

Including Betty.

In the aftermath, they told me Barlow himself had taken her down, trying to get to me before my fire blasted him one final time. But my heart knows the truth of the matter. I killed her. My magic killed her.

Or maybe it had just broken her heart, seeing me like that. I couldn't know. Blind rage is blind rage. There's no making any sense of things after an episode like that.

That's when I shut myself down and walked away. Walked away from the Association. Walked away from sorcery. I didn't want their psychologists, or healing. I didn't want their pity or support.

I sure as hell didn't want that kind of power anymore.

Crawling into a pit of a room for a year or so, I licked my wounds. Then I bounced around, taking jobs as they came by, before settling here, in this nice, normal place, with normal people tending their gardens, tinkering with their cars, and going to church on Sunday mornings.

A nice normal place where I could gather with normal friends who wanted to play a hand or two of cards and drink a beer. Maybe share a bottle of wine and hear a band. Take in the occasional ball game.

It worked for awhile. Until the nightmares started up, my magic tapping at the base of my skull, where the spirits used to whisper until I cut the cord. They were talking again in the only way they could get through, in my sleep. In my dreams.

And what they were saying wasn't good at all. It was filled with pain and darkness. Filled with light and fires that consumed. Something bad was going to happen and I couldn't stop it. Couldn't make it go away. Because they weren't showing me exactly what it was, or how to prepare.

The jukebox whirred and hissed, and Count Basie's piano hit the opening notes of "Lil Darlin'." Brass came in, smooth as anything. Basie always made me think of Betty.

I couldn't read the omens because I'd forsaken my magic. But I also wasn't willing to take it back. To rebuild my mind and heart the way Andre had rebuilt his nightclub. It wasn't that I didn't know how. I was just too damn afraid.

"Introduce us to your friend?" Carmine's voice brought me out of my reverie. I looked up. He and Bill were standing over our table, expectant looks on their faces. Of course they were. Rose Clemmons was a gorgeous woman, and one they hadn't seen around before.

"Rose, this smooth talker is Carmine, and the quiet one is Bill."

Rose held out her right hand, fingertips down, like she was royalty. Carmine cupped her fingers in his mechanic's paw. "It's a pleasure to meet you, Miss Clemmons."

"Likewise," Rose said. Then she flashed Bill a smile so bright he dipped his head.

"Ma'am," he said.

"You missed a good game today, Ronny. Bill here beat the pants off Louis and Jones."

I glanced over at the big table in back. Louis was gathering up the cards, laughing at something Jones had said. Good men, those two. Good men, all of them.

This whole joint was good. It didn't deserve whatever Rose was going to insinuate into the place, with her lilac bonfire scent.

"Rose thought she might have a story lead for me. We're just conversing here, to see if I'm interested."

In other words, back off.

Carmine looked like he was about to pull up a chair next to Rose, but Bill put a hand on his shoulder. "Let's get going, Carmine. I want you to look at that carburetor."

"Right. Nice to meet you, Rose," he said again. "Maybe catch you at the show tonight, Ronny?"

"Sure."

Turning back toward Rose, I realized I was sweating.

"You don't need to be so scared, Mr. McGee. I'm here to help you."

"You mind telling me why?"

For the first time, I caught a flash of nerves crossing her face. She took another sip of her drink, now mostly melted ice.

"Two reasons, I suppose. Maybe three." Rose looked straight at me then. "I know you've been having the dreams, Mr. McGee. I can feel them creeping under my skin. You tug at me."

You tug at me. That was a stab at my heart and my groin. A woman hadn't said that to me in a very long time.

"I tracked your suffering all the way here." Looking up at the bar, she signaled Johnson for a replacement G and T. "It's been a beacon for me for three months. Truth be told, I've been trying to avoid you, mister. But the pulling got too strong."

And my dreams had been getting worse. A lot worse. Malibu sliding into the ocean. New York City in flames. And those were just the things that made sense. There was a lot more that didn't. Fever dreams of strange armies marching across deserts, clad in white. The implosion of stars. I couldn't tell what was coming. And I couldn't tell what was just me.

"So what was reason two?" I asked.

Johnson picked up her old glass, setting the

fresh drink on the coaster. He set down some little napkins and a bowl of peanuts. "You good, Ronny?"

I forced myself to smile at his worried face. "I'm good, my friend. Thank you."

A group of men and women entered, calling to Johnson, smelling of ocean and sand. He directed them out back, toward the barbecue. The place quieted down again.

"Reason two?" I asked again.

"The Association wanted me to come. They've been picking up some static, and a few other folks are having visions. We'd like to triangulate the images and see what patterns exist."

My mouth set itself in a line. "You're from the Association."

She nodded. "I have been, for a very long time. Does that bother you?"

I just shrugged. Yeah. It did bother me, but I couldn't really tell you exactly why. Maybe I just wanted this beautiful woman to have come on her own. Maybe I was ready for someone to care about me again.

She leaned in close again, talking low. "Mostly, though, I came because of you, Mr. McGee. I came because I want to eat your suffering. To take it inside myself and make it my own. I want to turn your nightmares. To change them into the visions of a man of power. A man who can *help*." That last word was like the crack of a pistol.

I hadn't been a man who could help for quite a while.

"What do you mean, eat my suffering?"

"That's what I do, Mr. McGee. I'm a Suffering Woman. I eat your suffering. It's just fuel for me, and it dulls your pain. For some, that helps them heal. For a man like you?" Her face grew harsh, her mouth stern. "You have enough suffering in you to fuel me for quite some time. And I'm hoping that taking it on will shake you out of your self pity long enough for your to get off your ass and do the job the Powers made you for."

I just stared at her, wishing my head was clear. Wishing I hadn't had a beer and two bourbons. Wishing she hadn't just all but slapped my face, but ready for some more.

"I killed my wife."

Her eyes filled with compassion again, and she reached both hands across the table. This time, I took them.

"We both know that isn't true. Betty died fighting, because that was *her* job to do."

There was a tingling in my fingertips, and my palms started to burn. She was drawing the suffering out from me, memory by memory, inch by inch, as Cab Calloway shouted and stomped from the jukebox and the scent of barbecue came in from the back door.

The bourbon left my bloodstream. The memories of that night sliced through like knives and disappeared. The dog I had slapped across its chops when I was twelve. My father and his fists. All the betrayal. All the hope. All of my fears. She was draining them away. And Betty? God, the heartbreak and the beauty of her. All of it flowed out from me. The bastard Barlow. The seething hatred I'd kept simmering all these years.

And finally, the deep, deep, quivering shame of it all. That I had failed her. That I had lost it. That my magic didn't work. Couldn't work. Maybe had never worked.

All of that flowed from my hands and into Rose Clemmons, who grew sleek and plump and gorgeous with it all.

Finally, I drew a shuddering breath and the pricking in my palms grew calm again. It was just skin against skin, hands holding hands, companionably, across a wooden table in a Pasadena bar. I wanted to kiss Rose Clemmons' red, red lips.

I probed my head and heart. There she was, Betty, the way she looked when I first saw her. Smiling and strong, standing on a Los Angeles sidewalk in the pouring winter rain. Something in me sighed and relaxed. My shoulders dropped, and I sat back in my chair, sliding my hands from Rose's.

"Thank you."

Rose's face looked like a woman just after sex. Bright, soft eyes, relaxed mouth. She looked happy. Full. That should have bothered me, but it didn't somehow. I saw her for what she was. And she was just doing her job.

Maybe she was right. Maybe it was time for me to do mine. Or at least figure out what it was.

"Okay." I said.

"Okay?"

"I'll meet with the Association on Monday. You can tell them that. I want to figure out what all this means."

I shoved the bourbon across the table and stood up, then drank down the untouched glass of water she had brought me. "I've got to cover that concert tonight. I still have *that* job to do. And I'm not making any promises, except to show up Monday, and talk about the dreams."

Rose looked up at me, expectantly. "I will phone that in, Mr. McGee. But I have to put my bid in for you to come back to us. I hope you do."

"We'll see. Meanwhile, Miss Clemmons, might I buy you dinner before I have to get to the club?"

"Thank you for the invitation, Mr. McGee. But I'm not hungry anymore."

She smiled with those red lips of hers.

"Some other time, perhaps."

2

TO FORGET YOUR FORGETTING

Enrique wasn't some fancy pants accountant with a big house and slick car. He just did the books for mom and pops, the pawnshop, the boxing gym he sparred at, the botánica on the corner that dressed a candle for him on occasion, when he needed it, the last bookstore in the neighborhood, and some local restaurants. Restaurant work was his bread and butter, he liked to quip. Graciella, his daughter, groaned every time he said it. She was off at college now. He found that he missed her. She was the one who had marched him into the botánica one day, saying,"You need a candle, Papi. Let the lady help you."

A candle for love. A candle to ease his sore and aching heart. A candle, red, carved with symbols, anointed with oil from pink roses. He was to burn it every night and say the prayer she gave him. He felt damned uncomfortable about it at first, but he'd done it anyway. He hadn't said prayers in a very long time.

Once a month, he was to set out pink and white roses, as an offering to love.

In the years after Anna died, Enrique floated through the house. He smiled at his clients when he saw them, which thank goodness wasn't often, and then retreated home to his easy chair. Old cop shows. Belly growing softer, arms losing definition, boxing boots shoved in the back corner of his closet. Graciella would come home from high school and find him slumped over the desk in his tiny office room, it's sole window looking out over the crumbling concrete that held their trash and recycling cans, file cabinets stuffed full and piled high. His head would be in his hands, calculator and computer waiting for him to get back to work. He was never sure how long he'd been checked out. With the time lapses, sometimes it took him to midnight just to get through one day's work.

"Papi, come eat something. Get out of this room."

She would cajole him toward the kitchen where everything was neat as a pin, bright yellow walls, scraps of paper from some local cause or other stuck to the silver fridge beneath photo magnets of Disneyland, of Ernesto Ché, of Cesar Chavez and Dolores Huerta, and of Anna. Anna and Graciella. Anna and Enrique. Anna's face, beaming out of tiny squares, reminding him to live.

He hadn't wanted to. Not then. But there was Graciella to think of.

E nrique had showered off the stink from the boxing gym, slapped on some aftershave, and was en route to grab a late lunch before getting back to Cherish Grocery's accounts when he saw her.

She had stepped off of the sidewalk, perilously close to traffic, standing just outside a new sea green Prius and an old cream Volvo with a wooden roof rack. Those two cars were a snapshot of Berkeley, right there. Right hand gripping a walking stick with a shock of black feathers wrapped with leather around the top. Her skin was almost as black as the feathers. In all his life, he'd never seen someone so black. She was dressed completely in white: white long skirts, white long-sleeved shirt, white cloth wrapped in a tower on top of her head, framing her sharp face. Brightly colored beads roped around her neck and wrists. Her fingers were nobbed and ringless.

She was old.

He was just about to go offer her some help when he noticed she hadn't just wandered, feeble minded, out into the street. She was standing there with purpose, face turned toward the sky. Enrique followed her line of sight, searching, searching. Crows. At the very top of the Japanese plum tree.

The tips of his fingers began tingling, the way they did sometimes in the botánica. The way they used to, back when Mami and Papi told him stories of the ancestors and spirits, taught him how to read the shells and to offer oranges and flowers.

There was a strange scent in the air that he couldn't quite place. Copal? Sweet grass? He couldn't smell the usual coffee scent from the café he was heading to, that made salads towering with grated cheese and carrots, and round garbanzo beans. They always served it with a warm roll from the bakery down on 9th street. He loved those salads. Had been looking forward to eating one and closing out with an espresso made thick and sweet with condensed milk.

Despite his growling stomach, Enrique went still inside, trying to listen. It was then that he noticed: No one was pushing baby prams past him. There were no joggers. No people slept on the benches under the trees or sipped at tea, huddling over text books at sidewalk tables in front of the cafe.

There wasn't any traffic in the street. Two in the afternoon on a Wednesday. Spooky.

"I know you're there." She called out, voice raspy, and much stronger than he expected to emerge from one so small. Enrique stood dumbly, waiting for something to happen, knowing he was being rude. Mami had always taught him not to stare, especially not at his elders.

Slowly, her head lowered, and her shining black eyes leveled directly at him. "I was speaking to you, son."

Enrique moved toward her, uncertainty growing within him, along with the tingling and some strange pressure along his skin, and at his temples. Temples. He had never thought what a strange word that was to use for that place on the skull, that rested just behind the eyes.

She turned her attention back to the crows. He could see now that they were staring back down at her. Some strange communion was occurring. Walking toward her on the sidewalk, he felt his heart opening to light.

The first time Enrique had burned the anointed candle and said the prayer, he had felt both foolish and uncertain. He read the words off the little card the shop owner had printed out for him. Halting, the words came strangely to his tongue.

It was a prayer to heal his heart. At the time, Enrique was not certain he wanted his heart to be healed. It felt like a betrayal. Anna held his heart. Since the first moment he really saw her. Not the first time they met, but three months later, she'd come walking toward him, laughing, and something inside him felt changed forever. He'd been in love before. Several times. But nothing was like this. No one was like Anna. And then the cancer ate her brain away, taking their life together one memory at a time.

Those years had been horrible, but they had been better than the emptiness that followed.

He found, over time, that he grew to love the ritual of lighting the red candle, basking in the rose petal scent of it, watching the faint etchings in the wax slowly melt away, reforming into puddles, smoke, and air. He even grew used to saying the prayer out loud. The words came easier.

Over time, he felt that something in him eased.

"You got the payment, son?" The old woman was still staring up at the crows, two of them stared straight back at her. More were gathering each moment, chattering among themselves.

Then she looked at him. She looked at Enrique with her black, black eyes. She looked at him on that sidewalk, empty of all human life, except for him and her. And he wasn't thinking she was so human after all.

The air whirled around him, and he heard the sound of hands slapping the taut skin of a drum. Something was happening to his heart. Strengthened by the boxing, the running through the streets in the early morning, the lifting weights and eating lenguaje on Saturdays, and drinking red wine on Friday nights. Her night.

"But surely..."

The drums faded and she cackled at his confusion. "No. Nononono. I am not Her. I am only me. An emissary. Someone who lives between the Greater Spirits and you. I don't exactly work for no one. But I'm useful to some. Useful. To some. But I ask you still, you got the payment?"

He couldn't stop staring at her face. The small round chestnuts of her cheeks. The sharpness at the tip of her nose. The sharp planes of her jaw. And that tower of white on top of her head. She could help him.

"Wash me clean, Mother. Wash me clean."

"I'm not here to baptize you, son. That kind of

water, you're not ready for." A crow alighted on top
of her walking stick. "I believe I asked you a question." Now two sets of black eyes scrutinized him.
He shivered, feeling naked. Not knowing what the
answer was. What was the payment?

She began to walk toward him, stepping up
onto the sidewalk, stick tocking onto concrete. He
moved forward to help her, but she waved Enrique
away.

Reaching out her left hand, she touched his
breastbone. And he knew what the payment was.

Six months after he started working with the
candle, he was feeling better. Graciella had
stopped looking at him with concern when she
thought he was too occupied to notice. She smiled
when he ate the dinners they prepared in the
yellow kitchen. He started gaining weight back.
Found the boxing gym and began going there
during slow hours, not yet ready for the cama-
raderie of men, but needing to get out. To move. To
feel his strength again.

Muscles slowly built themselves. Women
started looking at him in the grocery store, or as he
sipped his espresso Cubano, lingering over the
news.

He wasn't ready for those women yet, who left
lipstick stains on the white porcelain cups, and
carried baskets down the grocery aisles in their

yoga pants, picking over lettuces and apples, and selecting single bottles of white wine. He wasn't ready for them, be they slim hipped or lush of body, be they dark skinned or pale. He wasn't ready for the men, either. Didn't know if he ever would be.

Graciella was enough company for him, but now she was gone, too, taking classes in calculus and colonial history, women's studies, and dance, working part time at the Rite Aid, stocking shelves. She had a young man, he suspected, though she hadn't really said. When she was home, it was mostly to study and to sleep.

Enrique started reading more books in the evening, instead of working until all hours. Amazing what being able to pay attention during the workday got a person: he actually got his work done in a timely way. Maybe he'd take a night class. Astronomy. History. Bonsai. Writing? Nah. Maybe.

The thing he really wanted to do? The thing he started doing in secret in the hours Graciella spent out doing who knows what? He started dancing. Merengue. Salsa. Mambo. His hips were rusty, but the more he moved them, dancing around the turquoise patterned living room carpet in his stockinged feet, the looser they became. He broke out the albums he and Anna had bought together all those years ago in record shops long gone. The albums were old when they got them, music from a different place and time. The old cabinet turntable they'd found one autumn Saturday at the flea market still worked fine, scratching out the tunes.

Herb Alpert. Willie Colon. The Buena Vista Social Club.

The sounds of brass and drumming filled the apartment. Enrique danced.

If he could have seen himself, he would have seen a man in flower, a man bursting with red, purple, and gold. He would have seen a man who smiled in the warm lamplight. A man in no need of wine.

He was sweating, damn it. He hated sweating after he'd cleaned up and was looking nice. And his stomach clenched. Not just nerves, but hunger.

"I don't know the answer you want." It wasn't really a lie. He knew, but he was uncertain. Or maybe he was just arguing with himself, the way he always did when it came to desire. To desiring anything but Anna's lips and laughter. To desiring anything but the touch of Anna's hands, and the words from that sharp mind of hers before disease stole her thoughts away.

The old woman didn't even glance at him this time, which he was thankful for. But she was walking up the sidewalk which made him nervous.

Where was she taking him? And where in hell were the people? There should have been college students on the streets, and teenagers getting out of school. Business women heading to the office supply store, or an afternoon foray to the gym. There was no one. Just Enrique, the old woman, and the crows.

How could he know what she wanted? And how could he offer it up?

He was not worthy. He had failed. He hadn't saved Anna. Hadn't even remembered that he could.

Dancing, he could momentarily forget he had the power. He could forget that he had not been told, but should have known anyway. He should have known that when his Mami spit the rum on the little potted figure made of stone, that it meant something. He should have seen it when his Papi lit the strong cigars.

He *had* known it, once. But had forgotten. He had forgotten so thoroughly that he didn't even recall that prayers were something that he had ever done.

He had watched Anna die and never prayed. Not even once.

Enrique sat by her bedside and lit no candles. He offered no water and drank no rum. He built no altars. He called no spirits. He had relinquished it all.

Curse his hands and curse the feet that drew

the power from the earth. Curse his mouth that could have spoken prayers. Curse his heart that should have known.

Seduced by numbers, he had given it all up even before he met Anna. Even when it became clear he was no genius in this world—just smart enough to be clever, and to understand, but not smart enough to discover something new emerging from the lines of the equations—his mind closed to the strange world of his childhood, though on family visits, his father always threw the shells, and his mother asked him to light the candles when they had extinguished themselves.

With Anna, life was good. Their dancing was just dancing. Their laughter was just laughter. It was clean, uncomplicated. True. It was as true as the mathematics he loved. She was the brilliant one: his scientist. His love. Who needed magic when he had Anna?

She had made it so easy to give up his family ways that he simply... forgot. He just forgot.

And he didn't think, even now, that Anna would have welcomed his prayers.

The old woman was leading him to a place he'd never seen in this part of the city, though it looked familiar. A cousin to the botánica where he now bought candles on his own. This place was darker, more uncanny. The old, white clad woman led him through the jingling bells of the chipped white door, into a room with an old metal cash register on the counter, and scales to weigh out the herbs and incense that crowded the wooden shelves behind.

There were books, too. And statuary. Beaded banners on what wall space was left. He closed his eyes for a moment. He *remembered* the banners. Yes. He had rolled them up in the old chest that he used as a bench at the base of his bed. His mother had sewn them in the evenings, while she talked to him of the Mysteries. He hadn't looked at the banners in years.

The shop smelled delicious, layer upon layer of scent: old wood, the sticky resin of burnt myrrh, white sage and rum. And weaving over it all, the faint odor of cherry tobacco.

"Follow me." She pushed through some clacking black and brown beads into a room to the left of the long counter. He stepped through.

A massive altar reached toward the ceiling. Red and white candles. Shining beads. Shells to burn incense in. Glasses and plates piled up with offerings.

The floor in front of the altar was old wood, whose veneer had worn away from years of feet shuffling forward and back, making their offerings.

An old man sat in a rocker near the altar. At first, Enrique couldn't even tell if he was real. His hair had white stripes like a badger's and he was sitting still. But then the brown eyes with their white sclera blinked.

"Welcome, son. We hear you gave up your gift and you've come to take it back."

The old woman nudged him forward with her staff.

"No. There's some mistake. I didn't ask for anything. She just appeared in the street."

The badger man chuckled. "You humans. You tell yourselves anything, don't you?"

Then Enrique remembered something else.

Over dinner last week, he had told Graciella he was ready for something. He had thought he was just talking about night school. Maybe—long shot, but maybe—dating someone. But the conversation came tumbling back into his head and he remembered what he said:

"I'm ready to feel like myself again. You know, when I was younger, I had dreams, visions of the way things could be. I was *interested* in the way things worked. It felt powerful when I figured things out. Excited. I could feel the power in my hands, like I could *do* something in the world. "

He had stood to clear the dishes. Graciella filled the sink with soapy water.

"You've done a lot, Papi. You raised me, didn't you?" She grinned over her shoulder as he scraped the dishes into the compost bucket and set them by the side of the sink.

"You are a smart and beautiful girl, Graciella, and I'm proud of you, mija."

Then he said it, the words: "But I wouldn't mind feeling powerful like that again."

"That's right, son." The old woman walked closer, staff *tocking, tocking, tocking,* on the floor. "You were the heir. You got that power. Your soul knows it all still."

He looked around the room. Confused. Something inside him felt excited. Another part of him wanted to cry. For the first time, he noticed a long, low altar lit with pure white candles. Glasses of water were spaced between them. Along with photos. Pictures of people well loved and long gone. The ancestors.

"Where are they, son?" He knew what she wanted then, this crow woman. This faerie creature. This witch.

He fumbled in his pocket for his wallet and drew them out. The photographs. Mami and Papi. And Anna.

"Put them here."

Hands trembling, he set the photos on the altar next to one unlit candle. The old man appeared at his side, holding out a book of matches.

"Light it."

Enrique didn't know if he could. He was suddenly shivering, as though the room itself wrapped him in a cloak of cold and silence. He longed for the sun outside this place of shadows. The candles, their beautiful flickering, suddenly only made him want to run.

The old man shoved the matches between Enrique's resistant fingers. He could swear he heard music. Those drums again, and a voice singing above the rhythm, songs of praise and longing. He ripped a match out of the book and scraped it against the narrow sandpaper strip. It hissed with light and sulfur.

He lit the candle. Anna's face reflected the yellow light.

"Beloved one," he said. And began to cry.

In the months that followed, his power slowly returned. He was learning how to forgive himself for his forgetting. Crow and Badger—who they actually were, he did not know, but this is how he thought of them—taught him how to say the proper words again. His dancing took on patterns of the old sigils of the greater spirits.

He unfurled his mother's banners and hung them on the walls. Graciella looked at the bright cloths, with their intricate beading and gave a sigh of contentment. He never even knew she had been waiting, but she had. Together, they built an altar to the ancestors in the westward corner of the living room. Other altars slowly grew in strange places around their home.

People in the neighborhood stopped Enrique on his daily walks to the cafe. They were having some money troubles. Did he have advice? Granny was sick. Was there a tea he recommended? Could he put his hand on their sick cat? Just in case?

Could he make prayers for them in the morning? Ask the spirits for them? Because he was closer to the old ways than they were, and they needed help.

After a while, Enrique stopped resisting. He remembered the things he knew once, as a boy: seeing sickness as a color, and hearing misfortune as a misplayed note. As the harmony within his heart increased, he could see what harmony looked and felt like in the people who sought his counsel.

The memory of Anna still hurt him, but even that eased, just a little.

He still drank his espresso with condensed milk. He listened to rock-and-roll, and the music of Willie Colon. He kept the books for the restaurants and stores, for the botánica that lived down the street, and got new clients, too. His wealth slightly increased.

"Not too much," said the old woman.

He needed to live closer to those who needed his help than the wealthy ever could. Besides, he liked things simple, and things were complicado enough.

He no longer needed the old woman to guide him to the shop that lived in between. He was learning different ways to call the Other City into his touch and sight. All it took was paying attention. He practiced that every day.

His feet still danced around the boxing ring, but his solo dancing in the living room only happened occasionally, when he was really happy. Mostly, he took that dancing to the club on Friday nights. He danced with women who had trailing hair and hips wrapped in skirts that swirled out like small galaxies when he spun them away from his body and back in again.

Enrique lit his candles and offered fruit and rum. The waters of healing baptized his soul, and he made friends with the crows.

Giving up his forgetting turned out to not be such a steep price.

His heart was growing strong.

3

A WINGED HEART

A FUTURE MAGIC STORY

A cascade of gray and silver oceaned from the sky. Clouds, shading dark gray to purple toward almost black, wrapped the city in a blanket of cold. The wet was expected to last the rest of the week, with warnings for the homes nearest the beach, who's waves Solana was certain matched the sky today, though she had been told by her foster to stay away until the rains stopped.

Oceans were unpredictable during storms.

She should have her forcefield up to repel the water. Her foster had made sure she had a good working system, but Solana enjoyed the feel of the rain sluicing her skin, and the smell of it rising from her coat.

Anything that she could feel like that was another sign that she was alive. She was thankful for that. She was even thankful for the pain in her right hip that never quite went away, caused by a slight limp from a knee that never fully extended itself.

She was thankful for the new boots with thick soles, and the extra long, forest green coat her foster had delivered just a week ago, knowing that the rains would come, and that Solana would be out walking. And that unlike normal people, Solana would be letting herself get wet.

Blue and white trams hummed by, casting the occasional spark. The noon. The twelve ten. The twelve twenty. She had credit for the trams, but her foster Michel and the court-ordered therapist both told her she should walk at least three klicks every day. The chip in her wrist would tell them if she hadn't.

Despite her hip and knee, Solana liked walking, though she pretended it was burdensome, which sometimes let her out of other chores. You know, for the sake of her health and all. She knew Michel and her therapist talked about how much to "push" Solana, and how much to back away.

She didn't mind that, either. Much. Sometimes it was tiring, but Solana knew she had things good. The therapist was a sandal – easy to walk all over – but Michel? He was actually a good person. Stang, even.

So Solana walked to and from her schooling sessions, and on free days like today, she walked to Main. She watched people. She composed poetry in her head, sometimes talking it into her com link to record for later, other times, repeating rhymes in her mind like an old rap-head, memorizing the schemes until she was home to tap it down.

Turning the corner, Solana walked down the strip of bright shops, restaurants, and the showcase rooms. Places where people could admire things in person before they debited their chips and had the packages delivered to their pads.

It had been raining steadily enough that the usual road smells had washed away. The air was clean, with the scent of lavender and mint, and of the rain itself. Solana breathed in deeply through her nose, closing her eyes for a moment, savoring the hush and the freshness.

Seagulls crested overhead, squalling and crying out like babies left too long alone in desolate apartments. She had a sudden craving for hot chocolate and wondered if she had enough on her chip to warrant the indulgence. She probably did. Michel was pretty stang about stuff like that.

Yeah, definitely stang. Michel wasn't too hard on the rules, and generous enough with sharing out the funds the gov doled out for Solana's keep. He made sure she always had some credit on her chip, and made sure her tram cred was current, in case she was tired of walking, or had to carry something home.

Or in case she needed to avoid her Da, now that he was out. And if he ever figured out where she lived, despite the court order.

They didn't listen when Solana said she wanted to see Da. Just kept repeating he was a danger to her. Like it was his fault she broke her leg and it went septic.

Like it was his fault she almost died.

"Out the way!" Shock slammed through Solana's shoulder, and she bounced against the rain slick hardness of a wall.

"Hey!" she said, old red brick scraping at her palms as she scrambled to catch herself on her complaining knee.

Sneaks slapping on the wet walkway. Two boys jetting past. A high whirring sped toward her. The Nabber car, dim red lights flashing, streaked after the running boys. Solana crouched against the wall, trying to catch her breath. The gray world contrasted with the sharp and painful focus of her hands, and she started laughing. She laughed so hard, she could barely breathe. Gasping.

And then she cried.

Slumped against the bricks, rain pelting her, Solana sobbed and fought to keep the panic rising in her belly at bay. They were just boys. Probably stole something. Just boys. The pain in her hands called to her, a fresh rupture in the gray-rain world and the distance she kept from far too many things.

Her hands scraped at the bricks. Again and again. Grinding. Tearing. Scraping off layers. Scraping off the lies. Scraping away the pain. Until the rain on her face brought her back home again. She stopped. Felt the rain and the tears all over her face.

She missed her Da. A lot. Scrubbing at her eyes, she felt the grit and sting.

"Crap." She'd rubbed brick dirt right into her eyes. Just great. Wiping her hands on her coat hurt, and now that she was back, she was afraid of grinding dirt deeper into the scrapes. Wiping her face with the arm of her coat, she struggled to stand.

She should wash her hands, get the brick dust out. May as well grab a hot chocolate, too. She deserved one, right, after almost getting knocked down?

There was a caf' just down the way, where kids from school met up sometimes, laughing, drinking coffees, studying, or just jerking around. She started moving toward it, then veered across the street instead, to a quieter place, more cramped. No one there she'd have to greet. She could retreat inside her bubble once again.

"I just wish..." she didn't even know. She told herself again, she had it pretty good. But things still felt hard.

She'd better dry herself off. Shops weren't too keen on people soaking their chairs. But Solana couldn't bear to let go of the rain just yet.

At least twice a season, Solana let herself get wet. Some years, that was a few times a week, if her schedule could stand it. The early years, after Da was sent away, she'd been too busy between schooling and gov meets, and needed to be dry. That was how things were before she placed with Michel.

People expected it of someone like her, to be dry and neat. Presentable, they called it. Actually, that wasn't true. People expected the opposite. They expected someone like her to be a ragged mess dragged in fresh from the road.

"To be respected by fools, you got to act like they do." Every time. Her Da was right about that one thing, despite the shitty mess he'd made of everything. Despite him being his own special kind of prayer-healing fool.

So mostly, Solana stayed dry and clean. Well spoken, too. Dry, clean, and well spoken meant higher class fosters. People of good will with broken hearts who wanted an errant teenager cluttering up their spare room with angst and noise.

The ragged-mess kids got ragged-mess fosters: a

moldy mattress and crap food. Crap schooling, too, if they got to school at all. Solana heard the stories of kids made to work molding ammo to stockpile, or raising a passel of baby fosters, changing dirty pants and mopping up vomit, all so the fosters could get some extra cash without working for it.

And she'd heard about the forced-sex, too, from the kids who'd been swimming the pool for awhile. Solana had been dead lucky on that count. Hadn't ended up with any freaks.

So she cleaned up her speech and kept herself mostly dry.

And hoped Michel kept her on until she could be out on her own without trouble from the Lectioners or Nabbers.

As she walked down the sideway, people who bothered to notice looked at her a little funny. She imagined what they saw: a plump girl with pasty white skin, blotched red from the cold, in a long forest-green coat, a sheet of gray and rain falling on her head. They would all be in their own little cubes of dry, wearing stylish purple suits, or hand knit sweaters, or even worker-clothes, more sturdy than the rest. But dry they would all be. Only the poorest got wet. Or poets like her.

Rain was for dreamers, not workers. And she really couldn't afford to dream. But some days, Solana keyed off her forcefield anyway, needing with a desperateness to feel cold moisture on her face. To feel something that seemed real.

After Da had been taken away, it was as if a

cocoon of spider silk had wrapped her up and
blocked her eyes and ears. Food tasted like dust
and she could barely hear the words anyone said to
her. She slept a lot. And when she wasn't sleeping,
she would grab small bits of pottery, or metal, and
slice into her thighs, watching the red well up in
narrow lines. Solana could breath easier then,
somehow. Like the feel of the rain pelting her body,
those lines of red told her she was alive.

Pain was always real.

It was Michel who suggested that Solana use
things like scent and texture to "anchor you to the
real" he said. He helped her plant rosemary in a pot
to hang outside her bedroom window, and brought
her fleecy blankets for her bed. One day when she
got home from schooling, there was a stuffed bat on
her pillow. Michel never said anything about it, but
Solana cradled it as she dropped to sleep, wrapping
its wings around one arm. In the morning, she
would find the bat resting on the pillow next to her
head, as though it had crawled up on its own,
finding a place for itself in the night.

Michel also badgered the gov for extra credits to
get her a "talk therapist" to help her with "grief
issues." Yeah. Pretty stang. Even though it was a
pain in the ass sometimes. The talk therapist was
pretty okay and actually helped Solana think things
through better. Helped her make connections
between things. When Solana's Da got taken,
they'd sent her to a psych who'd made her act
things out with dolls, which she hated, and put her

on drugs which muffled everything, which Solana hated even more.

So yeah, no drugs, and no cutting slices which left thin scars spidering her legs. Just walks. Plants. And rain.

Speaking of...She clicked on her forcefield to block the water, and boosted it with a little heat and air. Not enough to really dry her out – she didn't have the cred for that kind of a boost – but enough to make her just damp, instead of wringing.

The caf' was just ahead of her, warm golden windows glowing into the gray afternoon, arches framing what pastries were left after a day's worth of customers. Solana pushed open the heavy, brass bound door with her shoulder, and bells rang, announcing her arrival. The place didn't feel much larger than Solana's bedroom. Enough space for a low bar along one windowed wall, and four small, round, marble topped tables, antiques salvaged from some long-closed fancy restaurant, she guessed.

Solana unzipped her coat as the warmth of the cafe embraced her. Something inside of her relaxed.

Cinnamon, toasted sugar, and underneath it all, the smell of coffee. Solana looked wistfully at the flaky crust of a chocolate-filled croissant. No way did she have enough credits for a pastry and hot chocolate. If she was smart, she would get a black coffee, and load it up with brown sugar and cream.

But chocolate was what she was craving. Her

therapist told her to listen to her body and
emotions, to figure out what she really wanted.
Chocolate was it today.

The woman behind the counter smiled, bright
and sunny. Her skin was dark brown, warmed up
even more by the bright orange shirt she wore. She
was like the opposite of the day outside. Solana
wondered if the woman knew to do that on
purpose, or if that was just the way she was,
naturally.

"What can I get you?" She caught Solana's eye.
"That croissant is half off, since it's near the end of
the day."

"Just a hot chocolate. Please."

"OK." The woman pressed the screen inlaid
into the counter top, then looked up and smiled
again. "Make a wish."

Solana's brow furrowed. "What?"

The woman pointed to Solana's neck. To the
silver charm Da told her was her mom's. A heart
with wings, like it was ready to fly off her collar-
bone at any moment. Fly somewhere she'd never
seen before.

Solana shook her head.

"The clasp is turned 'round front. Right next to
the charm. That means you get one wish." The
woman smiled, a warm and gorgeous grin that
included Solana in it, just like they were old
friends.

Solana grinned a little back.

"Three credits for the chocolate."

Solana held out her right wrist to the scanner.

"Ouch. That looks like it hurts. You OK?" The woman's face lost its smile. Her eyes narrowed with concern.

Solana felt the red creep up her throat and stain her face.

"I'm OK. 'Z there someplace I can wash them?"

The woman nodded and waved a hand. "Back there. Your chocolate will be ready by the time you get back. Let me know if you need the med kit."

There was a door tucked behind an ornate screen, all black and gold, and painted with peonies.

Solana hung her coat on the brass hook screwed into the back of the door before she locked it. Looking at her face in the mirror above the sink, she was surprised the woman had even let her in the shop. She looked like crap, brick dust striping her pale face, streaked with tears and rain. Hair lank, plastering her head. Then she looked at her hands. They were ripped to shreds, with pieces of skin hanging off, and blood still beading up. Tiny bits of brick and dirt embedded in the cut.

Turning on the old water taps, she put an old fashioned stopper into the drain, then eased her hands below the water line, hissing through her teeth.

After cleaning the cuts as best as she could, she let the water glug its way into the pipes, and was glad to see that the toilet room had another old-fashioned thing: a paper towel rack. She ripped a couple off and patted at her palms.

Michel was going to explode when he saw them. She'd have to do extra sessions with Dr. Wong. Shit.

"Why'd you do it?" she asked her reflection. Her reflection told her she needed to wash off some grime. She carefully wet a towel and wiped her face. Her blue eyes told her nothing new. Just that she was messing up again.

Then she caught sight of the charm, sure enough, the little lobster claw hook nestled up against the winged heart.

What in the world would she wish for? To have Da back? To fall in love? To get through the next few years alive, and not having to move to a new foster? More money? Better grades?

What?

She bit her lip, eyes moving from their own reflection and back to the winged charm.

Solana whispered to her reflection. "I want to not hurt anymore."

Then, carefully, she turned the clasp back, so it rested on the small knob of bone, where her neck and back met right above her shirt.

"Okay," she nodded. "Okay."

Back in the caf', she slung her coat over a chair at one of the round tables and went to the counter where a cheerful yellow bowl steamed, swirls of cream and pale brown forming the shape of a small tree just on the surface. The woman behind the counter paused from cleaning the steamer, still smiling.

Solana reached for it, before remembering her hands. "I..."

"Oh no. I wasn't thinking! I can get you a mug with a handle, they just don't hold as much."

The woman paused a moment then, like she was thinking. A bit of silver winked at the corner of her left eye, where she'd pasted a small jewel. Solana had missed that before.

"Or if you're willing, I could try something."

"Like what?"

"I could try to heal your hands." The woman pitched her voice low, even though they were the only two people in the caf'. You never knew who was listening in. "I have a small gift. Not much, but enough for that," she nodded at Solana's palms.

The woman looked like she was serious. But that was just crazy. That was...what had gotten Da taken away. Him and his "church" with the laying on of hands in the "pastor's" basement room.

All that stuff wasn't real.

It had put Solana's life in danger. She'd almost died from fever, had been burning up for days. Da finally took her to clinic when she started shaking so hard she bit through her tongue. It was the blood that snapped him to, Solana guessed. She'd been too out of it to care. The throbbing in her tongue was about the only thing she was able to notice, her brain was so gone with the fever.

By the time the fever had cleared, her Da was

gone. They had taken him away. "Child endangerment."

She got picked up at clinic by her first set of emergency fosters. Then started the rounds of interviews. The shuffling. The trying not to look crazy. The speaking calmly. The hiding the cuts on her thighs.

Making sure the small shard of mom's broken tea cup stayed hidden in the pocket of her favorite vest, wrapped up so it wouldn't cut unless she wanted it to.

The woman in the orange shirt held out her own hands, waiting.

Solana backed away from the counter. "I don't think so."

She grabbed her coat and fled under the jangling bells of the heavy door.

"Your chocolate!"

Then she was back out in the rain, struggling back into the forest green coat, activating the force field without thinking.

Crapcrapcrapcrap. Solana clenched her hands, willing herself into the pain again. She didn't deserve the rain. Stumbling her way down the street, she turned toward the squalling gulls. One block. Two blocks. The brackish smell hit her nose as she walked toward the dunes at the end of the street. The rain was a sheet of gray meeting the churning ocean, white caps boiling and heaving. The wind turned her hair into coiled whips that struck her cheeks.

Cresting the damp sand, beach grass swishing at her legs, feet sinking, she walked toward the waterline and stopped. Turned off the force field. Held out her aching hands, palms up. Shredded skin met the benediction of cold rain.

A small prickle at her collar bone made its way through the wet on her head and the painful heat of her palms. The winged heart. Her wish.

Solana got to her knees in front of the roiling ocean, wincing as her weight hit her right knee. Stiff fingers undid her coat just enough to reach the charm. Touching one fingertip to the silver, she raised the other to the sky. Rocking on damp sand, she repeated the words. Three times, just like Da taught her.

"I want to not hurt anymore."

"I want to not hurt anymore."

"I want to not hurt anymore."

The ocean roared and pounded, but the rain began to ease, wind dying down. The charm burned beneath her finger, growing warmer, then it just...Stopped.

Solana took a heaving breath as rain pattered softly on her head. A wave of salt water came almost close enough to touch her knees. She should move back. But she wasn't ready yet.

The next wave touched her legs, salt water meeting her rain drenched coat. Solana sank back onto her heels, letting the ocean come. All the way back to her shoes.

Finally, it was deep enough. She moved her

hands down, carefully, and immersed her palms in the salt, salt sea. The water felt like ice crystals on her skin.

Her hands...didn't sting. The salt didn't hurt.

Scrambling to get her feet back under her, Solana got some space between herself and the ocean waves. Then finally, she looked down.

Her palms were pink and whole. The charm had worked.

She started to laugh. "Thanks Da, you crazy man."

Then she remembered. Her mom's face, leaning over her cot and smiling. The one image she had that was her own, not from some vid or picture. Solana's own eyes had seen her mother's face.

"Thanks, Ma," she said quietly, barely audible above the frothing ocean waves.

The rain slowed even more, finally stopping. Solana wiped the new skin of her hands across her wet face.

The gov wouldn't let her see her Da. Not for a few more years. But maybe by that time, it'd be okay. *She* would be okay.

She would know some things: like when to go to clinic, and when a charm would do. Like when it was safe to be near the ocean and when you needed to get away from the waves. Like when to use a forcefield and when you really needed to walk out into the rain.

And when it was time to get warm in a caf' with

a bright faced server who wore orange clothes, and could teach you some things about healing. Maybe.

Solana started walking. Steadying her feet on the sand, she realized that even though she was still limping, the pain in her hip was gone.

And she was ready for that hot chocolate now.

4

A LOAF OF BREAD FOR DEATH

V anth loved the feel of it, the dry, crackling edges of the crust, the resistance as she began to pull, the softness inside as her fists rent it in half.

She loved the taste of it. The wheat and yeast. The richness of rye. The crunch of barley.

And the fragrance. Warmth, and fire, and sunshine. A family gathered around a table, telling stories. The scent of home.

She'd had none of those things, not really, particularly not the last. Doomed to wander, she was. Forever.

Oh, she met everyone eventually, it was true. Every human being, at least. She looked down upon them, sometimes bending close to hear the final whispering hopes and confessions, regrets and dreams. Sometimes she shook their hands. Other times? Vanth watched as thousands, sometimes millions, were slaughtered, regardless of age or station.

She hated those times.

There were other endings, of course. Vanth tended to subcontract out dogs, and cats, and microbes, certainly. And plants? They had their own ways. But occasionally, an elephant or whale wanted to speak with her, and she made the journey to walk or swim at their sides.

The last non-human species she had paid a call upon was a massive tortoise. She had wanted to hear the secrets cached inside it's shell. That tortoise, Gordsong was its name, had shuffled off this coil at around about two hundred years of age. It had seen many interesting things. They had talked a long time that day, beneath the desert sun.

Stories were always the payment Vanth desired. For what was a world without them? Stories came from both imagination and from deeds. Some stories filled her belly with sustenance and fire, with the thrill of flight, or with the understanding of a thing long pondered. Other stories were briefly held, like sugar on the tongue. Every story had value. Vanth had a craving for them all.

But if she couldn't get stories, over the millennia, Vanth made do with bread.

She truly loved bread. If only people were more diligent in their offerings these days.

———

I really wished I'd worn gloves. Rookie mistake. You'd think I was a tourist or something. Huddling in my favorite old peacoat at the top of this windy hill, peering through gray swirls, eyes trained on the glow of a coffee shop one block down, wishing I was there, instead of here.

Yeah. My fingers could stand to be wrapped around a cup of black coffee.

San Francisco winters seem mild to those who live with sleet and snow, but the cold here is deceptive. I should know, I've lived here for twenty-three years, arriving from Florida when I was eighteen years old.

You know that phrase, "It chilled me to the bone?" That's San Francisco cold. The damp creeps in through every layer you own, through woolen coats, and scarves wrapped thrice around your neck, and those leather gloves you bought that the shopkeeper insisted came all the way from Florence, Italy, but you could have them at half price.

And then you left them on the dresser at home.

Yeah. That kind of cold.

And that's the kind of cold it was today, November 27th, in the no-mans land between American Thanksgiving and Christmas. Or the Winter Solstice, if you prefer. And I do.

My name is Harry Stegner, and I'm a psychopomp. Meaning, I help people when it's their time to cross over. "Death doula" is what some people are calling it now, but I don't care for that term. Doula is what you call a midwife's assistant. The word smacks too much of birth to me.

Death is not a birth. If you're very lucky, and subscribe to such beliefs, death is a going home. Other times it feels like getting pushed from a moving train. Sure, you can look at death as a transition, and I guess a romantic soul could call that a "rebirth."

I'm not. And I don't.

I'm practical about it. Everything has to die. We know that. The world is crowded enough as it is, without people refusing to leave the room, so to speak.

Where the hell was Vanth?

Hands shoved in the pockets of my pea coat, I peered through the gray mist that wreathed Powell Street as it sloped precariously down toward the bay. This wasn't the fat, rolling fog that streamed in off the ocean in the summer, rising from the water as it warmed. This was a creepy, spooky fog that hung in the air like a ghost.

God damn fog felt freezing cold, even though the temperature gauge on my phone said the air was only forty-eight degrees.

A cable car clanged by, half empty.

My phone also said she was late. Vanth was never late. If you could be in a thousand places at one time, would you ever be late?

Yeah. You wouldn't. Not unless you were a lazy slob, which Death can't afford to be.

———

They were out of her favorite rye at the Brooklyn deli. The baker, sweating in his fear, promised to make up a batch right away. He had it all ready, he said. It just needed to go into the oven.

Vanth had freaked him out when she showed up that day. She hadn't had a loaf of proper Jewish rye in ages, and the old man in the tenement up the road had just kicked off, with barely a story at hand. He had told her about the deli, though. His favorite place to eat. Came here every Monday, noon. Best rye bread in town. Put it on his tab.

Almost no one left her upside down loaves

anymore, except for children, playing at the table sometimes, until the most superstitious granny, the only one who remembered the old tales, flipped it quickly back again. Hoping Death hadn't seen it. That she would not be stopping by.

Mr. Moscowitz, though, he said there would be bread for her here, so she had chanced it.

The baker slid the giant wooden paddle into the massive oven, dragging out one dark and perfect loaf.

"It needs to cool," he said.

The smell hit her like a revelation. Like a deep, dark secret. A mystery made of flour, water, heat, and time.

"I'll eat it now," she said, then gestured to the loaf.

The baker wiped his nervous hands on a flour streaked apron, then picked up the loaf, juggling it a bit from palm to palm.

"No," she said, and gestured again. This time turning her upright palm downward.

He looked at her, confused.

"You have to turn it over. That's how I know it's mine."

_____

. . .

I wanted to meet her down around Washington Square Park, across from the double white spires of Saints Peter and Paul. I could've stopped at the place on the corner for a latte. Or better yet, a meatball sandwich. Either way, I would've been inside, out of this godforsaken cold.

But no, the windswept, mist crowded hilltop with the cable cars clanging by was the only acceptable spot in the whole, goddamn city.

I even tried to tempt her, dropping in a mention of rosemary focaccia from the meatball sandwich spot. Two birds with one stone and all.

But here I was, looking down at the black, steel banded face of my phone again. Definitely late. And no texted explanation. No Facebook message either.

That's a joke. Death hates Facebook. I do what I can to amuse myself.

"Come on…" I tapped my ratty sneakers on the concrete. Death was never late. Sometimes, much to my client's chagrin, she even showed up early. No matter what, though, like any good psychopomp, my job was to wait around.

"Tapping your feet, Harry?"

I whirled at the sound of her voice. Smooth as silk, that one.

"We had an appointment," I said.

"And here I am." She swept one perfectly manicured hand down her perfectly proportioned body. Black wool trousers, nicely cut. Black cashmere turtleneck. Dusky golden skin. Lush hips. Lips I would be tempted kiss if it wasn't Death Herself standing in front of me. Every psychopomp in the world is attracted to Death. Man or woman or something beyond or in between, she's always just our type. Shapeshifter? Or we just see what we expect? I don't know.

She says the skin tone is original though. Etruscan. I have no way to check.

Apparently, she'd taken over from some other Death-dealing-deity, and in another couple thousand of years, she'd hand the scepter over to someone else.

At any rate, I've learned three things in my years as a psychopomp.

One: Prepare yourself as best you can, because you never know exactly which moment you might get called away.

Two: Always take Death's word for something when at all possible.

Three: Make sure your bread is fresh.

Death *really* likes bread, and too often people forget this step. I think a proper offering eases the transition. Can't hurt, in any case.

You gluten-free, celiac prone people? You people on diets who clear your kitchen of any trace of starch? Figure something out. I hear there's a lot you can do by leeching the proteins out of the grains these days. I even tried some gluten-free challah recently. It wasn't bad.

"What are you doing here?" I blurted out.

"Tsk, tsk, tsk," Vanth clacked her tongue against her perfect, pearl white teeth.

Shit. I knew better, but the freaking cold was getting to me.

"Sorry." I cleared my throat, and dug my hands deeper into the pockets of my coat. "What I meant to say was...I didn't know we had an appointment. You know. Officially."

She arched an eyebrow at me. A row of cars whooshed by. Down the bay side of the hill, the cable car clanged, ready to make it's ascent back toward Market street. Every sound was muffled by the weird mist.

"I mean, sure we had *this* appointment, but I've got no one on the docket. Not until tomorrow, earliest, unless there's something you know that I don't."

It happened occasionally. A blood vessel burst when I was in the middle of lunch, and I missed the exact moment of death by a minute or two. I try to be good about that, though, and make sure that if I'm pre-occupied, one of the other local psychopomps is ready to stand by. There are ten of us in the City itself, and another hundred or so in the larger metro area.

We still sometimes get caught with our pants down, so to speak.

"No," she said. "No one's about to pop off in the next hour, at least, not one of your people."

The cold was making my right knee ache. I know I shouldn't be impatient with Death, but...

"So what gives?"

"I need you to do something for me."

———————

B ack in the the middle ages, people knew the value of life and death. Life was often cut short. You were lucky if you lived past the age of thirteen. If you were one of those who survived your early years, you had a decent chance of living to the old age of sixty or more.

Oh, perhaps you would get thrown by a horse and trampled. Or influenza would sweep through your village, taking three people out of five. Or you'd die pushing out your fifth child, taken by a hemorrhage.

Or you were caught stealing, or murdering, or poaching, or any number of sins.

In that case, the psychopomp on duty would stand near the gate of the prison, and the executioner would sharpen his ax, or make certain the rope was hung just so.

Vanth was very busy in those days, even though there were significantly fewer humans breathing in the stinking air.

The point of this story –never one of her favorites, but a story nonetheless– is that in that time, when bakers got ready to open their market stalls in the morning, they always set a loaf aside. That was for the executioner, who would not make it to market until long after the morning rush was done, leaving behind only the sorriest turnips, the rankest cuts of meat, and all too often, no bread at all.

The baker's assistant turned the special loaf upside down on the shelf, so the morning customers knew not to take it. Every hand steered clear of the upside down loaf. To do otherwise was to take a terrible risk.

It was bad luck to eat the executioner's bread, everyone knew that. You might end up next for the noose or ax. What people didn't know was that the executioner, in the secret of his room, always split the loaf in half.

One half was his, for dinner, or the next morning's breakfast, soaked in grease if he had it, or eaten dry before he sharpened his ax to go to work again. The other half? It was for Death herself, and would always, ever, be.

These days, executions comes via close range bullet, straight to the head, or in poison injected in a cold room at midnight, a handful of people watching through shatterproof glass.

The executioner can buy bread at any time of day now. There's no rush.

"You want me to ask every bakery in town to start turning loaves of bread upside down?"

I didn't voice the *Are you crazy?* But it was probably clear enough. She gave me another one of her Looks.

But I felt genuinely flummoxed. In all my years as a psychopomp, and in all my years living in a place where every freak and pervert was welcomed with open arms – because that's just how we roll – this had to be the weirdest request I'd ever had.

"I miss my bread, Harry. People are barely superstitious anymore. Science has taken over, and we old entities too often don't get our due."

"But the stories…"

She flicked her long fingers in dismissal. How in the world was she not even wearing a goddamn coat out here? I turned my collar up, still kicking myself for not bringing gloves.

"The stories are fine. Great even. But I really, really, miss bread. So many people don't even eat it anymore, which is a waste, if you ask me. What is more delicious than bread, fresh from the oven?"

It seemed as if she actually wanted a response to that one. I just shrugged. What the hell was I supposed to say?

"Yeah. Bread is tasty. But I still don't get what exactly you want me to do."

"It is so simple. The simplest thing. Much easier than the rest of your job. Just go to the bakery – you don't even need to visit all of them, just a few select bakeries – and put in a daily order for me."

"Of bread. That they can't sell. Because they're supposed to turn it upside down in the hopes that you'll show up and claim it."

Her face brightened. The mist cleared. The goddamn sun actually shone for one instant.

"Exactly," she replied. "I've got a particular hankering for sourdough."

———————

To make proper sourdough requires the right conditions. San Francisco has those in spades. The proper water. The right air. Some sprinkle of baker's magic that doesn't exist elsewhere. Go to Missouri sometime. Order sourdough. What they'll offer you will taste nothing like what you'll get in any restaurant or dive cafe in the City by the Bay.

Vanth wanted that. The Brooklyn rye had reminded her. There was nothing like the crusty edges and the moist, yeasty, air-filled pockets, of a top rate sourdough.

———————

I did what she asked, and got my two favorite local psychopomps to help me. Thank the Gods Death had backed off on asking me to visit every bakery. We met one day, over sushi, and discussed strategy.

Lifting the tiny cup of sake to my lips, I nodded along at the list Rebecca had going.

"Yeah," Raquim said, mixing more green wasabi into the little dish of soy sauce in front of him. "The place on Nob Hill? Their sourdough is dope. Best I ever tasted. We should ask them."

A grin lit up his dark face, pushing up his cheeks and wrinkling the edges of his eyes.

"Thing is," I interjected, "we've got our list, but what's our *plan?*"

"What do you mean?" Lisa asked, sweeping blond hair back off her pale forehead, and into a ponytail. I watched as she wound the rubber band around the thick, glossy locks. We were quite the trio. I was the scruffiest of the three, by nature. And the oldest, too. Made me wonder who would psychopomp for me when my time came.

I rapped my knuckles on the table, to scare off any listening gremlins. You never knew how news could spread.

Don't court Death. Not ever. No matter how gorgeous she is.

Raquim gave me a strange look. I stopped knocking on the tabletop and shrugged. That seemed to be my go to these days. Besides, someone had to keep the old superstitions alive. If more people had, we psychopomps wouldn't be in this dumb position.

"What are we gonna actually do? Waltz into a bakery one afternoon and say 'pretty please, would you take your best loaf of sourdough bread, turn it over on the counter, and not sell it? Yeah. We're saving it for Death. That's right. Oh, you want us to pay for that?'"

Raquim and Lisa were silent, and not just because they'd both taken the opportunity to shove both pieces of unagi into their mouths before I could get to it.

Damn. Barbecue eel was my favorite.

I poured us all more sake.

This was going to be a long meeting.

———

Vanth paced the Lagos high rise, walking past the sleek, sectional sofa, and the graceful wood sculptures, occasionally pausing to gaze out the floor to ceiling windows at the red and yellow lights of the cars driving by below. It was almost midnight, and the psychopomp wasn't doing her job. She was supposed to have prepared Mr. Oduwole to meet his ancestors. He was a very wealthy man, so the funerary celebrations to follow would be no problem. His family and children would be well taken care of.

There was no reason for Mr. Oduwole to resist the crossing. Nonetheless, breath still wheezed and moaned in and out of his bony chest, as his children wept around his bed.

No one but the psychopomp knew Vanth was even in the lavish apartment, of course. Only the most sensitive could feel Death, and far fewer could see her.

But this was getting ridiculous.

She wandered over to the kitchen, a white and gleaming place, with goldenrod yellow dish towels hanging from rods, and ochre red plates stacked in glass-fronted cabinets. A small feast had been set up on one long counter.

Vanth sniffed at the air, then stalked around the counter. There it was. Agege. A soft, fluffy bread. The kind of bread that squeaked between your teeth each time you bit down.

Sometimes agege came in loaves, but today? Laid out on a pretty, painted earthenware dish, were several fragrant rolls.

And one of them was upside down.

Vanth smiled.

Mr. Oduwole rattled out his final breath. His children shrieked and wailed. And Vanth reached out, taking the roll into her hands. Holding it up to her nose, she inhaled. It smelled of spring.

Then her sharp teeth bit down into the soft, sweet, bread.

―――――――――

My client was a kid. I always hated getting the young ones. Every week, it seemed, there was a teenager shot in the back, or some ten year old with cancer. You'd think after all these years, I would be over the heartbreak of it. But I'm not. It gets to me, every time.

The hospital stank of disinfectant, vomit, and piss. The antiseptic smell of isopropyl alcohol assaulted the back of my throat.

Sad Sack, the kid's name was. At least, that's what his friends used to call him, back when he had friends. Turned out he was a sad sack because a stealth sickness was slowly sapping away his life force. By the time the doctors figured out what it was, it was too late for anyone but me.

The job started pinging at me two days before, leading me here, to San Francisco General Hospital. A good place. But not a place you ended up if you were rich.

Sad Sack's parents definitely weren't.

I snuck into his room. The light was turned down low. Machines beeped, and breathed, and whirred. Someone had brought in a bouquet of lilies. The stink of them was almost overpowering.

The boy's parents, two women who looked careworn, older than they should have, huddled over the rails of the adjustable bed.

One of them turned, her eyes rimmed in red, ashy brown hair standing up in shocks on her rounded skull.

"Are you the chaplain?"

Good enough.

"Yes. Did you want to pray?"

The other, dark-haired woman, gave a harsh bark, as though her throat was raw from held back screaming. "It's a little late for that, don't you think, Candice?"

"Louise. Shh."

Candice squeezed the dark-haired woman's shoulder.

Then she looked at me, those red-rimmed eyes blinking in the dim light. "Would you pray for us? I mean, pray for our son? We...don't seem able to anymore."

"That's fine," I said. "I'm happy to pray on your behalf."

That much was the truth. Part of my job was to do whatever would help ease the path. Prayer was often part of it.

I looked around the room, and saw an abandoned food tray. I rolled it out of the way, to give myself a better place to stand. But really, I was looking, hoping, for exactly what I saw. Next to a half eaten plastic cup of chocolate pudding, was an untouched dinner roll.

I turned it upside down, then bowed my head.

V anth was pleased.

Somehow the psychopomps of San Francisco had managed to convince the bakeries to leave her offerings. It started with one man. French, of course. They were the first to have begun offering the executioners bread, after all. Next was an Italian woman, who had taken over from her grandmother. She was the closest thing to an Etruscan Vanth was going to get these days.

Both of them were superstitious enough to believe the strange stories Raquim, Lisa, and Harry had spun for them, some mishmash about selling funeral bread to their clients. That some of their customers wanted to set aside a loaf to feed the dead.

Then they turned around and told their clients that these three bakeries made special funeral bread, "in the old tradition." Exactly what old tradition? They didn't need the whole story, did they?

Word began to spread, and people began buying memorial loaves of sourdough to turn over at funerals.

"It's to feed the souls of the dead on their journey," the people said. "It's a custom from olden times. We thought it was a nice touch."

The psychopomps conveniently left out the part about the loaves originally being for the executioner. In most cases, there wasn't an executioner anymore, except disease and time. And the offering had never really been about them, anyway.

There was only ever Death. Vanth. She-who-walked-among-the-living.

And if you wanted her to pass you by? To not take you in her arms, the way she took Cousin Sally, or your brother Diego?

You gave her a loaf of the finest San Francisco

sourdough or Crown Heights rye you could make or purchase. And you turned it, crusty side down, on a painted plate, or a piece of white linen, or a countertop, or an old trash can lid.

Where you left the offering didn't matter. Death would have her due.

Vanth smiled, and inhaled the yeasty scent of sourdough, still warm from the baker's oven. At long last, she had her favorite bread again.

Freshly baked bread and stories. That was a good way to live.

5

LIZARDS AND LYING MEN

A MAGICAL ASSOCIATION STORY

The Sisters of Mercy came on the jukebox, Andrew Eldritch's voice crooning hoarsely over electric piano.

Dagger smiled.

Her deep purple lips and blue eyes reflected in

the floor to ceiling mirrors as she swayed on the old red carpet, skinny and naked except for a spiked necklace and the burgundy red wig that skimmed her white tattooed shoulders, tickling her collarbones.

Naked all the way down to her black patent leather platform pumps. Nothing to obscure the small breasts and subtly rounded hips. Just the way some customers liked it.

The beat kicked in, and Eldritch roared over the drums. Dagger whipped her wig around, and began to dance in earnest. Quarters chunked into slots on the other side of the small windows, as two of the reflective surfaces slid up and down, revealing men's faces behind the glass, framed by wooden grab bars set into the glass on either side. The other windows remained firmly closed.

The two other women on the shift danced and gyrated around Dagger, coming in and out of view, slices of reflection and refraction. Naked bodies revealing themselves from all angles, over and over, unto eternity.

The scent of industrial cleaner warred with cocoa butter, amber, lights on old carpet, sex, and the special scent of warm women's skin. This strange combination of smells had been Dagger's companion for three years.

How else was a witch-slash-sorceror-slash-psychic supposed to support herself?

Well, Dagger's Gran had an answer for that, but it wasn't one that Dagger was listening to right now.

The dancer named Casey Jones settled a striped railroad engineer's cap more firmly over her blond hair, and stomped black boots on the carpet in time to the drums before gripping the sidebars to assist the backbend that would display her crotch to whomever was lucky enough to be in the dark booth behind the glass.

The other dancer on duty, Ishtar, wrapped a red boa around her deep brown torso and picked her way to the other open window. Ishtar was as tall and lush bodied as Dagger was thin and sharp. Ishtar wound and twined the feathers as she moved closer to the window, flicking the ends toward the rapt customer on the other side of the glass before shimmying toward the mirrored back wall.

There was something for almost everyone within the glass walls of the Golden Drop, morning, noon, and night.

It was a Wednesday afternoon in late October, so the peep show was much quieter than usual, meaning the women could relax a bit, though continuous movement was still part of the job.

Dagger's feet weren't hurting even though her shift was almost over, which was a plus, and she enjoyed the hell out of dancing in a mirrored room with naked, gorgeous women.

Despite her pleasure at the pounding beat and wailing vocals, and the sight of her co-workers having fun, something she couldn't quite name was bothering her.

Something was always bothering her lately, especially since Gran's latest text message.

Dagger crouched toward one of the open windows and looked into the brown eyes of the man peering out at her. She smiled her purple smile again. His lips thinned into an approximation of a smile. Nervous, this one. Funny though, he wasn't "young and inexperienced" nervous.

This was something else. This was "middle aged and lonely and maybe insecure" nervous. The kind of man who'd taken too many hard knocks in life, and not gotten enough support.

Stray thoughts assailed her head. The perils of being a psychic who hadn't locked down her mind enough because she was preoccupied.

He'd lost his job today. Planned to pick up vodka en route home to his crappy apartment after he was finished at the Drop.

Shit. That meant Dagger should pay him a little kind attention, and not just zone out, working on whatever the problem was that itched at the back of her head.

Well, time enough for that once her shift was over.

Half an hour to go.

Dagger wiped sweat from above her lips with the tip of one narrow finger. And then she danced for the nervous man.

Two hours later, dressed in black jeans and purple Doc Marten's, t-shirt blindingly white under a black cotton jacket, Dagger sat at the long wooden bar of her favorite North Beach cafe, running a hand through her cropped white-blond hair. A small counter oven was fired up and roasting red pepper and eggplant sandwiches. Next to that, rows of bottles graced the wall. Pride of place though, was the large silver espresso machine that came all the way from Italia.

The cappuccino in front of her was proof of the machine's origins and the skill of Roger, who'd made it for her. It was just the right amount of bitter, smooth, and sweet.

Dagger stared down at her phone screen, chin in one hand, other wrapped around the brown ceramic cup.

"There is a disturbance on the æthers, Samantha. I'm worried about your mother," read the text from Gran. The text Dagger had looked at ten times already.

Yeah. Dagger would be worried too, if she could bear to think about Cleo. And if Dagger was the kind of witch who could do anything about a "disturbance on the æthers." But she wasn't.

Despite the psychic itching at the back of her skull that told her when something was off, Dagger hadn't done real magic in years.

She was still a witch, but she was the kind of witch now who stood under the full moon and prayed that someone would help her. She was the kind of witch who's friends asked her what herbs to use for cramps, or what amulet was best when they needed a shot of courage.

A witch's knowledge was something she still had. So were some of the small magics. But the big stuff? The real stuff? The stuff that took a direct connection to the chthonic forces and an Akashic library card?

Dagger couldn't do that any more.

"Is this seat taken?"

She smelled him before she saw him. Black leather and Polo Noir cologne. Yuppie biker. Not a bad combination, per se, though sometimes those types were a bit more arrogant than she liked.

Then she turned. Black hair curled around his slightly pointed ears. A barbell crowned the corner of one black eyebrow, silver contrasting nicely with his light brown skin.

"Go ahead," Dagger nodded, moving her messenger bag to the one of the hooks under the bar. Much as she liked her space, this time of the afternoon, it wasn't fair to hog two seats.

She ignored him while he ordered a Campari and soda, pondering a slice of the ricotta cheese-cake for herself, finally deciding yes.

Roger, the waiter/bartender/cappuccino maker set a brown plate with a slice of the creamy golden baked cheesecake in front of her.

"I don't know how you stay so skinny, girl," he said with a smile in his blue eyes. They'd had this conversation before. Roger was big, muscular, and a little soft around his gorgeous edges. He knew Dagger couldn't gain weight if she tried. And she had tried.

She scowled and picked up the fork he placed on top of a paper napkin and shook it at him. "Leave me in peace, Roger. I'm working!"

"Good thing, so am I," he replied, before winking and moving off to fill another order down the coffee bar.

At least she had the money for food now. There'd been a year or so where she just didn't have enough money to eat all the time, and refused to take any help from Gran.

That was the time before she discovered she could dance naked in a room full of women and get paid decent money for it. Her body still hadn't put back on the weight she'd dropped then. Weight she could never afford to lose again.

That was a scary, shut down, time. Cheesecake and cappuccino were much better than that.

What did Gran expect her to do, though, Dagger thought, as she sliced a corner of cheese-cake off with her fork.

Oh, all the Powers, that was good. Not the dense, too sweet cream of the refrigerator cheese-cakes from her childhood. A baked ricotta cheese-cake was light, a little creamy, and just the right amount of sweet. Crumbs tumbled across her tongue, chased by the milky espresso.

"I saw you dancing," the voice next to her said.

Oh, just great. Dagger knew she shouldn't drink her coffee so close to work, but damn it, she liked Luigi's, the little Italian cafe across from the park from the gray church.

She looked around the tiny cafe, searching for an empty seat. The man place a hand on her arm. She whipped her head back.

"Get your hand off me," she growled.

His eyes widened and his fingers leapt off her jacket like he'd been bitten. Good.

"I'm sorry. I..."

"Just leave me alone," Dagger said. She saw Roger look their way, a question in his eyes.

The man held up his hands. He wore a silver ring set with onyx on his right pointer finger. The hands sticking out from his leather motorcycle jacket looked square and soft. Like he'd never picked up a wrench in his life.

Damn yuppies, wanted to look tough, but never wanted to do the real work required. They paid other people to keep their image up for them. He probably didn't even have a bike.

"I'm not stalking you..."

Dagger raised an eyebrow.

"Well, not for that. I mean, not that you don't..." he shook his head. "I need your help."

"I just bet you do," she said, standing up. Damn it. She was really enjoying that cake, but there weren't any open tables anywhere.

His voice dropped. "Not that kind of help. I need magic. Someone told me you worked at the

Drop, so I went to see you, but you left after one song, before I could say anything."

The back of her head was quiet. No buzzing meant no immediate danger. Okay. Dagger sat back down, and leaned down the wooden bar. "Roger, keep an eye out, could you?"

"Sure thing," he called back.

"I didn't see you at the Drop," Dagger said.

The man shifted on his bar stool. "I. Uh. Must have been in the two way mirror booth."

Just great. Must have been. As though he hadn't chosen that booth on purpose, with all of the other empty clear-glass booths available that afternoon.

"What do you want?" Dagger asked. "And what's your name?"

"I'm Chet." He held out a hand. She ignored it. He picked up his Campari and soda, acting like she hadn't just given him the cut. "I'm in trouble."

"Isn't everyone?" Dagger asked. Shit. She was so going to have to call her Gran. Right after she heard this yuppie biker out.

"You're going to have to buy me another cappuccino," she said.

Three cappuccino's later, and the slice of cheesecake demolished, Dagger was no closer to figuring out what the heck the yuppie – Chet – actually needed.

She was going to have to take down the mindwards she'd erected after encountering that lonely man at work. Reading Chet's body language and listening to his jumbled story wasn't enough.

"Order me a meatball sandwich, will you?" Dagger asked. "And a Stella. I'm hitting the loo."

Chet nodded, white lipped. His easy confidence had left him, though he still couldn't tell Dagger what the heck was scaring him so much.

Though he had managed to tell her how he'd found her. It was her ex, Tomàs. The two men had met on one of the big Sunday biker rides down the coast, and gotten to be friendly enough that they went out drinking together one night.

When Tomàs was drunk, he talked. And the fact that he had very recently broken up with a stripper who also knew magic came tumbling out. Jerk. Dagger couldn't be too mad at him. She actually still loved Tomàs. Missed him, even. But he pushed her too much to be something that...she just couldn't be anymore.

Dagger squeezed past the tiny tables against the windows that looked out onto the park. The sun was westering, lighting up the spires of the church as it headed toward the bay. It was getting later than she liked, which meant she was going to hit rush hour on the train.

Two dudes in loose jerseys played an epic battle on the foozeball table, bent fiercely over the pegs, jerking the blocky little men this way and that, trying to score.

Dagger snicked the lock on the bathroom door

shut, washed her hands, and looked at herself in the mirror. Her short blond hair was spikier than usual, which meant she'd been tugging at it without noticing. Her eyes looked huge. Dark. A little scary.

Something was trying to come through. Something she was trying to damn hard to ignore. Something that wanted to show her...that something bad was coming.

Dagger didn't want to see it. Didn't want to hear it. Didn't want to taste it.

But with the text from Gran, and this yuppie showing up at her favorite Italian cafe, and the itching turned to knocking at the base of her head, where skull met spine, Dagger was going to have to just deal.

She didn't want to deal. She didn't want to give in to the rush of information Tomàs and Gran had been imploring her to take in, to transmute, to offer to everyone who needed it.

Dagger turned one of the old fashioned spigots and bent toward the rust stained white porcelain sink. Splashing water over her face, she tried to cool herself down. It didn't work. The brown paper towels were rough against her skin.

How long could she stall in here? Why had she told Chet to order her a damn meatball sandwich? She could have just shoved her way past him, and gone out the door, running down Broadway toward the train before he could pay and unlock the helmet from his bike.

Her pocket buzzed. Gran again, texting. "Samantha, you can't avoid me forever. The Association called a meeting and I want you there. Stop whatever it is you are doing and come home." Even texting, Gran used complete sentences.

By "come home", Gran meant home to the Association of Magical Arts and Sorcery. Home to the legacy Dagger gave up when her mother died. Home also meant Gran's Pacific Heights Victorian, where there was a permanent room set aside for Dagger. She hadn't stayed in that room for a long time.

Oh yeah, and of course Tomàs was an Association member too, though he was on probation for "sharing too much information with non-mages while intoxicated." People like Chet.

Okay. Okay. Dagger drew on the Air around her, calling up the barest whisper of her Element. A slight breeze ruffled the edges of the brown paper towels in the metal holder. She opened up her mind. Chet was still there, starting to wonder what was taking her so long.

And there it was. The image of a monster in his mind. A large creature, flickering between a lizard and a man. The same type of creature Dagger's mother had died fighting.

"Damn."

Running wet fingers through her spikey hair, Dagger dried her hands again, unlocked the bathroom door, opening it to the sound of foozeball, conversation, and the smell of savory meatballs, warm between panini on the tiny oven grill.

Her stomach growled for the first time in months. She may as well eat dinner on Chet's dime. And have that beer.

And get him to tell her honestly how the hell he'd ended up being chased down by the Lizard Men.

She should probably call Gran at some point, too.

The following week, Dagger was back at the Golden Drop. She was closing. Her least favorite shift. Frat boys and sailors in town for Fleet Week, along with boys fresh from several rounds of alcohol at the bars down the street. Sometimes male/female couples would come in, sharing the bigger corner booths. Or a crew of lesbians out for some fun.

They were always a kick. Dagger loved dancing for the people who had nothing to prove, who just wanted to enjoy themselves and clearly hoped she was enjoying herself, too.

And her regular customers were great. The big black man with kind eyes behind his glasses, who wanted to discuss science fiction in the tiny breaks between songs. The white guy covered in tattoos who was always respectful, asking how her day was going and then chunking a dozen quarters into the metal slot, keeping the window open as long as he could.

She needed to be able to space out a little, and think of Chet and whatever these Lizard Men might want. Dagger had gone through every book her mother had left behind, but she hadn't found much. There were snippets and possible threads that needed weaving together. Or more than likely, some flash of insight that came from nowhere.

But there wasn't really time for the slow, pleasant, lazy undulations and far off musing gazes tonight. Dagger had to be lit up, and on, much as she hated it.

Tonight was full on frat night. Boisterous groups of jerks from Stanford and UC Berkeley, pounding on the glass, drinking from contraband flasks, and flashing money through the windows. As if she would ever go anywhere with any of these dudes, let alone have sex with them.

Dagger had asked security to remove two groups of men already, and it wasn't even midnight.

Three other women were in the mirrored room tonight, and all of them were busy, dancing from window to window, leaning in to blow a kiss, pinch a nipple, flash what was between their thighs, and wink before twirling out to the middle of the red carpeted floor.

Casey Jones was on again tonight, in full sexy railroad worker gear: striped cap, black boots, and suspenders holding up a matching striped skirt that didn't cover a damn thing. Ishtar was off because she had night classes on Wednesday's. She was doing a Masters in history.

Jessica and Colubra, both new, were filling in, gyrating and laughing, not annoyed by the frat boys at all.

Give them time. Once their freshly purchased vinyl waist-cinchers – green for Jessica and red for Colubra – started to lose their sheen, their smiles would grow a bit strained when the entitled jerks came through.

It happened to all the dancers, eventually. Every job, no matter how enjoyable, had its problems.

Two and a half more hours before Dagger could strip off her burgundy wig, throw on jeans, and ask the front desk to call her a cab. She was starting to sweat, and moved toward the giant fan attempting to circulate the sluggish air around the mirrored room.

Dagger could have raised a breeze on her own, and had started practicing again after parting from Chet on Monday night, when she'd headed to her shared flat for a long phone call with Gran.

"Safety first, Samantha," Gran said. "I don't care how mad at the Association you are. Your mother has been dead three years now. It's time you got over it…"

"Got *over* it?" Dagger spat into the phone.

Gran sighed. "That isn't what I meant. I'm sorry I said that."

Dagger was silent, barely able to breathe.

"She was my daughter, Samantha. I miss her every day. But life has to go on."

"I'm living."

"Yes. You are. But not well, working in that *peep show,*" Gran spat out. Dagger could almost feel Gran tugging on the front of her elegant gray sweep of hair in frustration. Another family trait Dagger had inherited.

"You could be using your gifts," Gran continued. "We need you to take up your responsibilities again."

Mad as Dagger was, she had to admit Gran was at least partially right, though considering there were burlesque dancers in their family history, she needn't have been so dismissive of the peep show part.

So Dagger dusted off her meditation bench, rummaged through a drawer for some candles, and took herself through her paces. Slow the breathing down. Drop the focus deeper. Raise enough of a breeze to blow out a candle flame without using her physical breath.

After a few day's practice, she could call the winds again without getting a headache, but she still had work to do. Dagger wasn't quite ready for full time witch work yet, either, so here she was, dancing in her platform shoes again.

Then she saw something from the corner of her eye. Something that didn't look quite like a man. The back of her skull started buzzing.

"What the?" The mirrored panel next to her descended. But she could have sworn...

The panel raised again, and a giant lizard face leered at Dagger from behind the glass.

Its eyes glowed red.

Whattodowhattodowhattodo?   Dagger gasped for air, trying to inhale the sweat, sex, cleaner, vinegar, amber, carpet smell as deep into her lungs as possible.

It wasn't making it through. It felt like all the air had been sucked from the room. She looked about. The giant fan still whirred in the doorway and the other women laughed and danced, bending toward the windows, and twining around each other.

They were fine.

The mirrored panel whirred down again, hiding the lizard head from view.

"I'm..."

"Dagger, you okay?" Casey turned, hanging from the wooden bars that framed the window she danced in front of, one foot propped on the window's edge, arching her torso backwards. Even asking a concerned question, Casey knew how to entertain.

"I think I'm going to be sick." Dagger ran as fast as her platform heels would take her, across the hideous red carpet, shoving past the fan.

She had to get out of there.

Thinking fast, she stumbled down the narrow hallway, toward the dressing room, with its giant makeup mirrors lit with marquee lights, tall padded stools, and a bank of battered red lockers. The dressing room was empty. No one on break, and, since it was the last shift of the night, no one prepping to go on. A roll of paper towels and spray bottles of vinegar sat lonely on the counter next to abandoned tubes of lipstick.

Fumbling at her locker, she struggled to get her shaking fingers to open the damn combination lock. The ever present dressing room smell of vinegar calmed her down somehow.

What should she do? She couldn't call security to kick the lizard out. And she shouldn't be throwing magic around in the peep show. But what the hell should she do? Call Gran?

Ripping off her wig and taking off the damned platform shoes, Dagger hopped around her locker, slipping on underwear, socks, black jeans, a loose blue tee shirt. She flopped down on the ancient sofa crouching along the back wall to pull her boots on.

Gabrielle, the sleek manager, a former dancer herself, leaned in the doorway, neat as a pin in a pencil skirt and tasteful blouse and pumps.

"Your shift isn't over," she said, frowning.

"I'm sorry, I feel really sick. Almost threw up on stage."

Gabrielle just stared at her, sure that she was lying.

"You can't just walk off, Dagger. You were supposed to check in with me."

"I know. I know."

Dagger stood and grabbed her messenger bag from the locker.

"But I really need to go now, before I puke all over the place."

Gabrielle stood aside, letting Dagger through the narrow door.

Dagger would probably get her shifts cut back. Maybe even get fired, though that was less likely as this was her first offense.

But really? She didn't even care.

Racing toward the front, she entered the shadowy customer area, with its dark lattice patterned carpet and the booth doors lit up with dim red lights. Rows of orange bulbs glowed from the ceiling.

The music was tinny out here, quiet. Men's voices called and bellowed out front toward the entry desk. She could hear them, and didn't look forward to running the gauntlet. Damn. One drawback of leaving the late shift before the customers had been cleared out.

The particular ell of the hall leading toward backstage was empty, just one lonely door with a small red lightbulb above the frame.

Was the Lizard Man still in there? Dagger paused outside the door to the booth and reached a little with her magic, trying to feel what was there. The image of rust colored rocks and the taste of dust filled her mind before the door slammed open, knocking her against the wall.

Just as quickly, a man in a dark suit had his hands around her throat. She couldn't breathe at all. Thrashing, kicking, Dagger pushed back against the wall, trying to get leverage. Trying to pry her fingers under his thumbs to take the pressure off her windpipe.

Her boots kicked at solid shins and battered up against the wall behind her.

Where the hell was security? Surely she was making enough noise to call them.

She stared at the man's face, pasty white lit by red and the dim amber hall lights. Narrow face. Large straight nose. Hooded dark eyes.

Then she was staring into the red eyes of a Lizard Man. Then pasty white skin again.

Damndamndamndamn. She squirmed harder, jerking her shoulders back and forth, pounding and kicking her boots, as she formed her fingers into a hook, yanking hard on the hands gripping her throat. Damn it. She couldn't break the seal.

His face was shifting faster and faster, lizard to man, man to lizard. Dagger needed air. And she needed it now.

Gray spots danced at the edges of her vision. If she didn't call up some air soon, she wouldn't be able to call anything.

"Gran!" she tried to shout with her mind, sending the image of a Lizard Man as far as she could. No telling if it would get through.

Dagger reached toward the night outside the peep show walls. To the street outside, all honking horns, taxi cabs, and drunks walking past neon signs, singing to the sky. Air. There was air out there. She pulled as hard as she could, drawing it toward her, filling up with her Element, even though she couldn't draw a breath to save her soul.

Air insinuated itself in through her nostrils, and the pores of skin on her face and hands. Not enough. It wasn't enough. She pulled harder.

The man slammed her head against the wall. She heard security shouting. Finally. Finally they noticed.

Then she was gone.

Dagger came to with her face pressed into filthy carpet and Gran's voice talking with some man. Greg. The security guy who must have saved her.

"It was wweird, ma'am. This man was chchoking Dagger against the wall and then..."

"Yes?" Gran was asking.

Dagger realized she could breathe again, and carefully inhaled. Her throat felt crushed. Bruised and painful. Even drawing in breath hurt. She tried to lower her attention deep into her body, away from the pain, and directed the air to soothe and repair the broken blood vessels and ease the bruising.

She'd still have visible injuries, for sure, but at least her magic could speed the process.

Greg was still talking, hemming and hawing. Stuttering. She'd never heard him stutter before. Gran must be making him nervous.

"He chchoked her and then r-ran. I ccouldn't stop him."

Dagger cracked an eye open to see. Sure enough, though his bulky, handsome frame towered over her Gran, Greg was shaking.

Gran's pale hands were moving in the dark space, asking Greg to continue. Her variegated gray hair was a gorgeous sweep that angled out from her chin, barely brushing her plum shantung silk clad shoulders.

Damn. Even at a mid-week midnight on an emergency call, Gran looked perfect. Dagger knew it was part magic and part Gran-has-a-lot-of-money, but it was also just...Gran.

"Ouch," Dagger said, trying to lift her head off the disgusting carpet that was crawling with Powers knew how much bacteria.

Greg bent to help her sit up, which set her head pounding like a...

Gran stood over her, lilac scent enveloping Dagger, soothing her head. "Do you need the hospital?"

"No. Please no."

"Alright then," Gran said. "Young man, would you please help my granddaughter to my car?"

Tucked into a blue velvet armchair in Gran's vast Victorian living room, with huge bold contemporary canvases gracing the white walls above the wood wainscoting, Dagger slowly sipped at warm chamomile tea with honey. Even that mild brew felt like ground glass going down her abused throat.

Gran sat on the button tufted blue and cream damask sofa across from her, in the corner nearest to the fire, cut glass tumbler of whisky in her hand. Her feet were tucked beneath her, flexibility a sign that she still trained in Pukulan several times a week. Strong as Dagger was, she wouldn't want a physical altercation with Gran.

Gently massaging her throat, Dagger considered another sip of tea. It wouldn't be a bad idea for her to take up martial arts again, considering how badly she'd botched tonight's encounter. Lizard Man was taller, heavier, and had been waiting, but that was still no excuse for Dagger to have let him lock his hands around her neck.

"Are you going to practice being a witch again?" Gran asked. Really, the family were sorcerers. But Gran's mother hadn't liked the word. Plus, they were all conversant with Tarot cards, crystals, using brooms to clear negative energy, and all that other witchy stuff, unlike "real" sorcerers, that rarely touched the stuff.

"Do I have a choice?" Dagger rasped.

Gran smiled wryly at that. "It doesn't appear so." She twirled the whisky in her glass for a moment, then looked Dagger in the eyes.

"Samantha, I want you to quit that job and move back here. We have work to do, and I can't hunt down Lizard Men and protect you at the same time."

"Okay. That's fine, Gran."

Gran looked startled at that. Dagger supposed she'd grown used to expecting a fight. Dagger rested her head on the back of the chair, suddenly exhausted.

"Can we talk about this tomorrow, Gran? I've got to get some sleep."

Dagger started to stand and the living room window exploded.

As glass shards sprayed inward, Gran ducked and rolled from the couch, hands lifted, sending up a wall of glimmering energy, blue as the ocean. Everything paused for one second, before a BOOM cracked the living room and the shards reversed their course.

Right into the gaping jaws and red eyes of the two Lizard Men climbing in the bay windows.

The lizards shrieked and strobed, man to lizard, lizard to man. Dagger managed to get behind the velvet chair and struggled to call up Air. She wasn't sure what help she could be here. Gran seemed to be handling it well.

Sirens were dopplering toward them.

"Do something about that!" Gran shouted to Dagger, still holding the Lizard Men at bay.

Dagger ran outside, planted her feet in the patch of lawn in front of the towering sycamore tree.

Streetlights cast giant tree shadows on the houses. In a flash of white, an opossum scurried off to shelter.

Refocusing her mind, Dagger did the first thing she could think of, not sure if it would help or not.

She called the wind.

Dagger pulled so hard a gale force almost knocked her on the ground. All the trees on the street began to shake and moan. Car alarms were screeching from the wind buffeting parked cars.

Dagger focused on the tree in front of her, funneling the wind to move one giant branch that reached toward the cream and purple Victorian. The limb swayed, groaning with the strain. The wind was relentless. Dagger made it so.

She pushed and pushed with her mind, feeling her own resistance wanting to push back or give up, crumpling with the strain of it.

And then something deep inside her, the something she'd held at bay since the Lizard's choked out her mother's magic, rose to the surface, suffusing her with the scent of winds that precede rain. The freshness of spring. The siren song of winter.

Dagger became the air. All this effort? Unnecessary.

She smiled into the night. All she had to do was flick one finger to the left, and the wind would do her bidding. For now, at any rate.

Dagger lifted her right hand, flicked her ring finger toward the mighty branch. It cracked. Broke. Ripped. The wind shoved it at the bay window, smashing the Lizard Men against the frame.

Looking up, Dagger saw Gran approach the window, hold out both her hands, and fry the dangling bodies with her fire. They disintegrated before Dagger's eyes, leaving behind the broken window. The tree limb creaked and groaned, then fell back onto the grass.

Dagger stilled the winds, right as three police cars screeched to a stop, fanning out around the house.

Well, there was that to deal with now, but at least they had a plausible explanation.

And this crop of Lizard Men were gone.

Dagger and Chet were back at the cafe, this time huddled around a two top table near the plate glass windows looking out over the park. Gray clouds hovered above the gray stone church across the way. The trees were losing their leaves.

She could come here without worrying about customers bothering her anymore. The day she went to quit, and clear her wigs and shoes out of the battered red locker was the same day she got fired. Convenient, that.

"How did you get involved in all this?" Dagger asked. "How did the Lizard Men get to you?"

This had been confusing her. Usually magical beings kept to themselves, only attacking other folks with magic. The Association made sure to keep magic on the down low as much as possible. So how did a normal guy like Chet end up afraid, and asking for her help with something like this?

Lizard Men weren't the small magics, the "can I get a spell or some herbs to help my ailing dad?" or "will you read my Tarot cards?" Lizard Men were the real deal. The stuff that normal people should never, ever, have to encounter.

Dagger's cappuccino was good, just the way she liked it. Roger made sure of that, every single time. She nibbled at a raspberry ring, crunching through the white sugar crust into the firm pastry below.

Chet drank an Italian soda, raspberry liquid sending bubbles upward in a tall pint glass. He traced swirls into the condensation on the side of the glass with one brown finger.

"How did I get involved?" he asked.

Dagger didn't bother to respond, just sipped the creamy foam from the top of her coffee and stared at him, green eyes steady over the brown ceramic cup. She held back a wince. Her throat was mostly healed, but still felt a little raw.

Chet coughed and looked out the window as though the answer was hovering over the park.

Or maybe he was staring at his own handsome face in the glass.

"I was just riding my bike down Folsom one night and these lizard guys stepped out from an alley. I swear, I almost crashed."

"And then what happened?"

Roger dropped a stack of cups behind the bar. They shattered on the tiles. Cursing ensued.

Chet ran fingers through his dark wavy hair.

"I'm not sure I can even explain it..."

And then Dagger got it. She saw the thing she should have noticed right away. That ring on his hand wasn't just a pretty biker bauble. The onyx was a focusing stone. For Elemental Earth.

"Damn the Powers," she said. "You're a sorceror, aren't you?"

Chet quirked one dark eyebrow, then let out a breath.

"Trying to be," he said quietly, looking back down at the raspberry soda. "But I got in over my head."

Dagger sat back in her chair, plunking the cappuccino cup onto its matching saucer.

"You jerk. You big damn jerk. You weren't going to tell us, were you? And you weren't even going to help, were you?"

He started waving his hands in the air, as though to ward off Dagger's anger.

"No. No. I would have! No way did I expect them to come for you so fast!"

"But you did expect that they would come."

Dagger's voice was quiet. Barely audible over the hiss of the cappuccino machine, crockery being swept into a garbage can, and the voices all around them.

Chet's face grew a shade paler. He nodded.

Dagger stood, scraping the wooden chair back with her thighs.

"Well, I don't like people who lie to me and then put me in danger."

Dagger slung her black jacket on and tugged her sweater sleeves down. She stared at him, this man who had come asking for help. This man she thought knew nothing, and had gotten caught in magical cross fire somehow. Turns out that he had drawn that fire, and then sent it her way.

Threatening her, and worse, threatening Gran.

Dagger gave him one sharp nod before slinging her bag over her shoulder.

"Don't expect us to help you again," she said. "We're witches. Sorcerers. Not the damned Salvation Army."

Then she pushed open the clanging door and walked out into the gray and cloudy day.

She'd take battling lizards over lying men. Any damn day.

READ AN EXCERPT OF BY EARTH

It was Solstice Eve, the longest night, and the coven had gathered. It was the time that ancient people thought the sun stood still in the sky before reversing itself.

Some said it was the night the sun would be reborn.

So much in her life was uncertain right now; Cassiel welcomed the moment of stillness and the promise of rebirth. Twenty-two years old and healthy, with a pretty enough face and a mass of curly red hair people admired...on the surface, Cassie's life looked pretty good.

Inside, though? She was worried all the time.

The slanted walls of Raquel's attic were painted creamy white, including to the knee walls. The dark planks of the fir floor gleamed in the light from the candles massed on altars in each corner of the space. Nine people sat on bright cushions in a rough circle.

Raquel was not only a coven mate, but Cassiel's boss at the café. A regal black woman with dreadlocks flowing down her back, Raquel looked around the space, making certain everything was ready and in place.

A clap of her hands set a row of metal and beaded bracelets snapping on her wrists. Two more claps, and Cassiel felt her attention snap itself in place along the column of spine. She felt the rest of the coven exhale around her, and exhaled, too. Ready for magic. Ready for the night.

Raquel gestured toward the center of the room and Moss, a slender Japanese American man in his early twenties, picked up his athame, a double-bladed witch's knife, and began slowly turning in a circle. Cassie felt Moss's blade sweep by her, causing the edges of her skin to prickle and stand at attention.

She could almost see the blue flame she'd been told was the vital energy of magic, and of life itself. Prana. Mana. Essence. She certainly imagined it now, snaking from the blade tip as it traced the edge of the circle.

When he reached the place he had started from, the blade swept up in an arc overhead and then back down, forming a glowing sphere, a sphere of safety, a sphere to focus, a sphere of protection for those within and those without.

Cassie let her soul wander deeper. She let herself open to the magic of the night.

"Cassiel, is your cantrip ready?" Brenda said. The cantrip. The poetry that helped tune magical operations and rituals. Cassie was a poet, and the coven had started looking to her to weave spells of words.

Brenda had been Cassiel's main mentor for the year and a day of her coven apprenticeship. The white woman was in her early forties, with a messy array of brown hair piled on her head. As usual, she wore a flowing tunic over slim pants. Tonight's tunic was black, shot through with purple stars. A chunky silver pendant at her breast reflected the candlelight.

Cassie smoothed her hands on her jeans, tossed the heavy fall of red curls over her shoulder and stood.

Stepping forward to face the north, she said "By earth…" She turned, pointing to each cross quarter in turn, charging up the energy, speaking as she went. "By flame. By wind. By sea. By moon, by sun, by dusk, by dark, by witches' mark..."

Cassie felt the energy build as the words moved through her. They were simple words, but like all magical poetry, their very simplicity increased the potency. What mattered was that they focused the witch's will. What mattered was that they called the planes of existence closer together, joining above and below, within and without.

"...We consecrate this holy ground, with sight, and sound, and breath twined 'round. With will and love, from below to above..."

Cassiel felt as if the whole hub of the cosmos spun around her, within her, and then locked into place. "Let the magic portals open," she said, then stood, vibrating in the hushed, still center of the space for one long breath. Then she bowed and took her place in the circle of the coven once again.

"So mote it be," eight voices responded.

Two other coveners, Alejandro and Lucy, carried a small table and a large black mirror into the center of the circle. The buttoned-up IT guy and the house painter, tall and short. Alejandro saw the future, and Lucy did a lot of work with the ancestors. Those two couldn't have been more different, yet their magic fit together like dusk mirroring dawn.

"Tonight we scry," Raquel said. "We look into the other worlds to see what we can find there. We ask for guidance for the coming year. We ask for help. We ask for visions of what may be, and visions of that which must fall away, and we ask on this, the longest, darkest night, to feel the promise of new light. So mote it be."

Cassie was drifting in and out, between the worlds of matter and æther, feeling the weight of the longest night around her, feeling the magic in the room. She felt a sense of home, as she always did when surrounded by the Arrow and Crescent Coven. She could taste that sense of home, just like she could taste the mulled wine the coven had toasted with before heading up the stairs. The memory of it slept on the back of her tongue.

But she also had to admit the sense of home wasn't as strong as it was before, because even though she still let herself float in the in-between, her anxiety was back.

Cassie watched her coven mates move in and out in groups of two or three to kneel in front of the big black polished mirror, gazing into it, seeking prophecy or reassurance, a way forward or a way to release the past. She realized she was scared—terrified, actually, and growing more frightened by the minute.

The things that were in her past were things she had hoped to keep buried—the ghosts clamoring for her attention, day and night. The inquests. The police calling her for help on cases. Her fourteen-year-old self, shaking and stammering as she tried to testify on a witness stand, testify to things that no one should ever see. To things that no person except murderer and victim should ever know.

Except the victims were ghosts. And Cassiel could see them. Could hear their terrible stories, and see the images of their murders all too clearly in her head.

The ghosts were the reason she fled Tennessee.

"I can't do this," she whispered, "I can't, I can't do this."

Raquel moved towards her, put an arm around her shoulders. Her friend and boss drew Cassie in, and cradled her against her chest for a moment. Then, with a squeeze, she released her and turned Cassie's face toward her with her fingers.

"Cassiel," she murmured softly, "you are a child of the Goddesses and the Gods. You are beloved of this coven, and of the Goddess Diana herself, and we will not forsake you. Whatever it is you see tonight, I will personally help you bear it. You can do this. You got this, girl."

Cassie still felt the tension of sickness clamping down her throat and churning the mulled wine into a sour liquid in her belly as she nodded.

"Guess I'll get it over with," she said.

She moved forward with two other coven mates, Alejandro and her best friend in the coven, the elegant Selene.

She watched as they bowed their heads, gazing into the black expanse, Alejandro's face forming a sharply backlit profile. Selene's face was obscured by a fall of straight black hair. Then she leaned forward herself.

Staring into the black mirror was like staring

into the curved bowl of space. Cassiel remembered nights out in the wilderness of Tennessee, coming upon a high place, nothing but black night and stars, so many stars, the kind you couldn't see in the city, the kind of stars she hadn't seen in years. Closing her eyes for a moment, she took three deep breaths and looked once again into the mirror. She saw the glimmering wink of candles, and the dark reflection of her own face. She saw a hand reaching out as though in friendship. She saw her parents. Her grandmother.

Feeling tension rising in her shoulders and belly again, she willed herself to calm down and drew in another deep breath.

"Help me see," she whispered to the mirror, "help me see what I need to see."

All of a sudden the mirror was wiped clean. There was nothing. Just blackness, deep, deep blackness. Cassie leaned in further, trying to keep her eyes soft as they wanted to focus, trying to find anything, something. "Show me, please." And there it was—an image of a burning tower. Cassie gasped and rocked back on her heels.

"No, no, no, no, no," she said.

She felt Raquel next to her. "You're fine, girl. Anoint yourself and look again." Raquel was holding out a small blue bowl of water.

"I don't think I can," Cassie replied.

Raquel was silent, still holding out the bowl. Cassie shook herself, dipped her fingertips into the bowl, then bathed her face and ran damp hands through the top of her hair. She lifted the heavy fall of hair and placed one cool, moist hand on the back of her neck and breathed.

It felt good. "Thank you," she whispered to Raquel, who nodded and moved back again.

Cassiel evened her breathing out and leaned toward the black mirror once again. Her eyes unfocused and Cassiel dropped into the black mirror. She was flying.

Flying through stars, flying through the air, then steering her spirit lower.

She was flying above the city of Portland and then she saw the room that her coven was in—she saw Alejandro and Selene, still kneeling by the black mirror, the other six lying down or sitting in a circle around the altar. She saw that some of them had left their bodies, shimmering silver cords attaching their spirits to their flesh.

She saw her own silvery cord and followed it down. It was as though her spirit were in two places at once, the observer and the observed. Cassie watched herself gazing in the mirror, and felt things go black again.

And then her eyes opened on to the face of a beautiful black woman with the strong, tall body of a warrior, a small tape recorder in one hand and a pen in the other.

"Who are you?" she asked.

"Who I am is not important. I don't exist here anymore, except as memories, ambitions, and work that

still needs to be done. I need you to finish it because he can't. He's not able."

"Who? Who can't?"

The woman just shook her head.

"Follow the tower on fire."

"What? I don't understand. What do I need to do?" she asked.

The woman just looked at her with firm eyes, then scribbled something on a piece of paper.

"You will know," the woman said. *"Tell Joe I still love him. And tell Darius I said hi."*

The woman held up the piece of paper. Cassiel peered at it, trying to make out the word.

And then the woman was gone.

FREE BOOK

Visit thorncoyle.com for a free short story collection and to sign up for a monthly newsletter.

If you enjoyed this book, please consider telling a friend, or leaving a short review at your favorite booksellers or on GoodReads.
Many thanks!

ALSO BY T. THORN COYLE

Fiction Series

The Panther Chronicles (Complete)

To Raise a Clenched Fist to the Sky

To Wrest Our Bodies From the Fire

To Drown This Fury in the Sea

To Stand With Power on This Ground

The Witches of Portland (complete)

By Earth

By Flame

By Wind

By Sea

By Moon

By Sun

By Dusk

By Dark

By Witch's Mark

The Steel Clan Saga (2020/2021)

We Seek No Kings

We Heed No Laws

We Ride at Night

ABOUT THE AUTHOR

T. Thorn Coyle has worked in diverse occupations, and been arrested at least five times. Buy them a cup of tea or a good whisky and maybe they'll tell you about it.

Author of *The Steel Clan Saga*, *The Witches of Portland*, and *The Panther Chronicles*, Thorn's multiple non-fiction books include *Sigil Magic for Writers, Artists & Other Creatives*, and *Evolutionary Witchcraft*.

Thorn's work appears in many anthologies, magazines, and collections. They have taught magical practice in nine countries, on four continents, and in twenty-five states.

An interloper to the Pacific Northwest U.S., Thorn stalks city streets, writes in cafes, loves live music, and talks to crows, squirrels, and trees.

Connect with Thorn:
www.thorncoyle.com